LADY OF DEATH: THE COMPLETE
CASES OF MR. STRANG, VOLUME 1

LADY OF DEATH
THE COMPLETE CASES OF MR. STRANG, VOLUME 1

CARROLL JOHN DALY

COVER BY
C.C. BEALL

POPULAR PUBLICATIONS · 2022

TABLE OF CONTENTS

PAROLE

*Meet Mr. Strang—the Strange and
Terrible Crusader Against Crime's
Latest Outrage, Parole!*

1

ANOTHER BODY

INSPECTOR JAMES BARTON stood looking down at the body. The cameramen were taking shots. The finger-print experts and the boys from the ballistics bureau were still going about their work. The medical examiner had shaken his head and muttered that it was a brutal bit of business and it was fortunate he had a strong stomach. His parting words did not make Inspector Barton feel any better. They were:

"Lower salaries and more labor for the medical examiners! You inspectors might give a little thought to the overworked medico. After all, my job does not begin until the corpse has presented itself, riddled with lead, or simply cut and hacked to pieces like this poor woman here. It's too bad the police are not hired to prevent crime rather than to punish the criminal."

Dr. Farrington cleared his throat as he reached the door.

"You keep the body tied up and expect me to do a good job. Don't ask me how long she's been dead. Fetch the body downtown and I'll give you one of those medical guesses which the papers publish as profound wisdom."

Sergeant Fox made a grimace after the doctor left and turned to the inspector.

"I found her just like you saw her, tied up there in the

*A knife protruded
from his chest*

chair. She was tortured to make her talk and gagged so she
couldn't. It was a horrible end and a slow death. She had
information someone wanted. I'd say they didn't get it!"

"Why?"

"Well—the slow death. She didn't die from any single
knife wound. She was slowly hacked to death; just passed
out in the agony of torture."

"But the struggle, man—the struggle! These chairs
knocked over; the bullets in the ceiling. Look at the plaster
on the floor! It doesn't seem as if such a frail little woman
could have—"

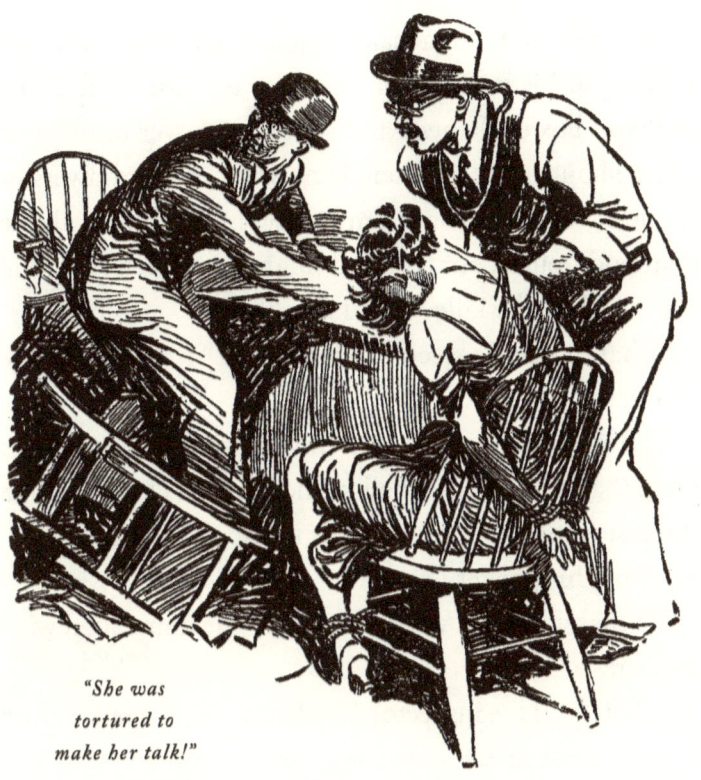

*"She was
tortured to
make her talk!"*

The sergeant pointed at the locked closet door.

"The story may lay there. Cassidy could yank it right off its hinges. I don't see why he doesn't."

"You don't, and I don't, either. But the defense made quite a point of a smashed door in the Regan case some years back. Jansen should be along in a minute with the locksmith."

"Here, you!" Barton called to a cameraman, "You got a picture of that closed closet door. We'll want another one after it's open."

He turned. The lettering on the office door read simply:

NORRIS ADAMS

"The superintendent said he was a diamond salesman. Didn't put his business on the door because he feared a stickup," Fox explained. "I've sent a man over to the post office about his mail. There is nothing in the drawers of his desk but blank paper. I'm getting in touch with all the diamond houses, but this bird might have been handling hot ice. Think he killed her? I don't know."

"That's right," agreed the inspector. "You don't know. But here's Jensen!"

The locksmith looked with disgust from the plain brass plate that housed the small keyhole in the closet door to the inspector, dropped his tools to the floor, and jerked a key from his pocket.

"Is that what you wanted opened?" he demanded with a sneer.

"That," said the inspector, "is what we want opened. And since it seems so easy or you're so damned smart, you might do it with gloves."

The locksmith, so sure of himself a few seconds before, saw the body, trembled violently, and had trouble slipping on the rubber gloves and more trouble getting the key into the lock. The inspector waved back Sergeant Fox's offered assistance.

"He's our expert!" he said with irony. "He's got to qualify as an expert in the witness box. And whatever we find in that closet, if anything, is evidence A, B or C, and must be so accepted by the court. No plant by the police, no manufactured evidence that—God in heaven! Fox, grab him!"

This last outburst as the locksmith finally got the key in the lock, gave it a sudden twist. The door flew open.

THERE WAS NO need for Fox to grab the body that stood

upright in that closet, for the dead man was not tumbling out. He was supported by an iron hook, the collar of his jacket deftly twisted about a coat hanger. The knees sagged slightly, for the man was tall and the closet had a low ceiling. The handle of a knife protruded from the center of his chest.

The inspector stepped forward. He took in the sleek black hair that was matted across a slightly yellow forehead. He saw the bulging, staring eyes; eyes that were glassy and sightless. Nodded his head when the sergeant suddenly echoed his thoughts aloud.

"There's terror in his eyes, Inspector. Not just agony, like that in the woman's. He saw it coming and didn't like it. I wouldn't be surprised if this was the lad who tortured the woman and—"

They both saw it together, and the inspector hid it from the others with his broad shoulders. It was not just the hilt of the knife that suddenly caused both the officers' heads to jerk back. It was the thing that the knife held to the dead man's chest; the blood-soaked bit of paper with a faded newspaper photograph on it. Though the wet, smeared print was hard to recognize as bearing an exact likeness to the dead man, the caption under the picture was clear enough and strangely free from blood:

Leonard Faine. Sent to the state's prison for a particularly brutal murder in 1931; released on parole today. Another human vulture turned loose to prey on society. *Correct the parole evil.*

"Faine! Yeah, sure. Faine!" The inspector failed to hide

the agitation in his voice. "I think the knife with the paper on it was driven into his chest after he was dead. The man was shot once." He lifted the dead man's head slightly, slipping the sogged paper easily from the blade. "There, right behind the ear. We'll say nothing about the clipping!" And when Sergeant Fox would have voiced a question, "Police business. Important evidence! Don't yap about it!"

The reporters were slipping into the room one by one. Halerhan, of the *Record*, was the first to view the body. He whistled softly. "Leonard Faine! Ran his mug in our sheet a few weeks back. Another paroled convict, by God! Why— what the hell, Inspector! Why shove me back?"

"Talk to you later, boy!" The inspector whispered the words through the side of his mouth. And then louder, "There, there, boys; don't tramp all over the room!" He stepped to the door, passed through and out into the hall.

Halerhan, at his heels, murmured:

"Another parole violator, eh? Was it Faine who croaked the girl? But who killed Faine and hung him up in the closet? Now, now, Inspector! You know the *Record* is backing you up for Commissioner of Police, and the way you've been catching paroled convicts—the mayor will have to appoint you. Come on! Let's have it!"

Inspector Barton's weatherbeaten face seemed to take on a darker shade of brown.

"AND, JIM"—THE REPORTER became both familiar and confidential—"there's something screwy about the whole business. Don't try to scowl me down! I'm no cheap hood; I'm your friend. What's this talk of someone who knows the underworld well, putting the finger on paroled prisoners who really should have lived and died in stir? Well—

that lad in the closet knocked over the girl. Some bird came in and caught him at it, didn't like it, and stuck a knife in his chest. Simple enough!"

"So you've got it all figured out, eh?"

"Sure," Halerhan nodded. "There was blood in the hall, wasn't there?"

"You learned that, too! So what?"

"So the killer of Faine carried away a bullet with him… Come on, Barton! The old man's against the parole racket. Why not open up? He'll smack that pan of yours all over Page One. Don't be just a dumb cop. Talk!"

"Exactly what do you want to know?"

"Who killed Faine—if you know."

"I don't," Barton said flatly. But he wondered if he did know.

"Well, you've put your finger on a bunch of killers lately; nearly all of them turned loose from jail as good, honest citizens who needed only another chance in life. Where do you get your information? Does anyone give it to you?"

"Of course. The police system is a great machine. It's many ramifications and sources—"

"Hell! I don't mean that. I mean—just one man. The one man, for instance, who tucked his knife away in Faine's chest."

"Good God!" said the inspector. "You're not suggesting that I'm encouraging murder!"

"Not murder, perhaps. Faine tortured the girl. This lad who hasn't any use for such a pastime, he's impatient with paroled convicts who immediately take up their old trade. So he just naturally knocks Faine over in the course of an exchange of lead, hangs up the body in the closet and puts a knife in his chest."

The inspector was tempted to put a big fist in the reporter's stomach and start him backwards toward the stairs. But he didn't. He liked Halerhan; and besides, the *Record* was behind him in his effort to show up the entire parole system and "shoot the boys back to jail" almost as soon as they came out.

"There must have been a reason for the knife. You know, Inspector. He didn't have a pin handy, so he used a knife. Used it to pin a message on that chest—a message that—"

"Nonsense!" The inspector laughed, turned as he saw Doctor Farrington coming in the door, walked over and joined him.

"Don't tell me, Barton. I know. One of your cops strangled himself trying to untie the woman," the doctor said.

And twenty minutes later the medical examiner added, in answer to Barton's request for advice:

"Advice? Certainly! Throw up a couple of windows. It's a small room for two stiffs."

2

BARTON MAKES A VISIT

INSPECTOR BARTON SURVEYED the dark, empty street for some minutes before he crossed it. He slid, more than just stepped, into the entrance of a walk-up apartment. He didn't hesitate there in the lighted hallway. His right hand came out, and without breaking his stride his finger found and pressed the bell of apartment 5-D. His finger had hardly left the bell before the lock clicked steadily. Barton entered a dimly lit hall.

He paused at the foot of the stairs for some moments, but no one sought entrance behind him, nor did anyone come down. Then, running a hand across his forehead he hurried down the narrow hall, peered behind the stairs and even shaded his eyes with his hands as he looked through the smeared glass into the darkness of the stone court behind.

Slightly annoyed at his own suspicions—not nervous-ness—for he didn't admit having nerves, he turned and went rapidly up the four flights of stairs.

The door of apartment 5-D opened just as his hand reached for the knob. He passed down the narrow hall. He heard the lock snap behind him and the rattle of a chain as it fell across the door. Then he stepped into the living room, picked up a chair with its back to the wall and halfway between the heavily draped windows and the entrance door.

He wasn't over friendly or even pleasant to the man who had let him in, when that man spoke:

"After this, Inspector, I'd come directly up and not loiter on the ground floor."

"You're telling me my business, eh?"

The tall man in the white servant's coat bowed slightly.

"I was simply suggesting, Inspector, what I was told to suggest by Mr. Strang."

The inspector's mouth opened for a sharp retort but the words never came. What he finally said was:

"I damned near didn't come at all."

"I know. You have doubts. I sometimes wonder if it is your idea of right that makes you hesitate to come, and if it's your ambition that finally drives you here. You are hardly a man who'd come out of simple curiosity; and certainly you are not one who would betray—or, in the parlance of the underworld—rat out on a man who is risking his life every minute of the day and night to make you a police commissioner."

Barton reddened slightly.

"You don't talk like a servant. More, a—"

The man grinned.

"I *am* a servant, though, and I was graduated from Harvard in '29." And with a smile as Barton mentally made a note of the university and the date, "I am lying a bit as to the name of the college and the date. I am sure my master would object to your valuable time being wasted in gathering information about me that would serve no useful

purpose. May I bring
you a drink?"

Inspector Barton
shook his head. The
man turned to leave.

"Just a minute!" The
inspector held up his
hand. "You have a
name, I suppose. I see
you now and then. It
might make things less
awkward if you told it."

Inspector Barton

The servant bowed from the waist.

"My name," he said, "is Maxie."

"Hell!" said Barton. " 'Maxie' doesn't fit you at all."

"Perhaps," said the man, "that is the reason I am called
Maxie. You will carefully lock the door after me, not forget-
ting the chain. And if I may suggest it, do not take too
official a view of the master's latest activity. I have read the
late editions of the papers. There is a feeling that even if
Leonard Faine had spent twelve hours of agonizing death
in that closet, justice would not have been fully meted out
to him."

"Yes. Quite so!" It was not hard for Inspector Barton to
be indefinite. His superiors had taught him that habit and
its political value, over the years. "I'll be seeing you again,
Maxie."

"Most certainly, if you call again within the year and
nothing untoward happens to me in the meantime."

"Within the year! What do you mean?"

"Within the year I will be dead."

"Dead!" the inspector gasped.

"Yes, sir. Quite dead."

IT WAS A full minute after the outside door slammed closed that the inspector followed Maxie into the hall, turned the catch and snapped the chain back on the door. Then he returned to the living room, removed his gun from its shoulder holster and thrust it in his jacket pocket.

After over twenty years on the force, Barton had jumped from lieutenant to inspector in eighteen months. There was no doubt in his mind that this strange man he was waiting for was entirely responsible for that quick promotion. The name of and the evidence against every sensational criminal Barton had taken or who had been shot dead resisting arrest had come to him directly from this man, who called himself Mr. Strang.

And every one of these criminals was a parole violator. Yes. One man was responsible for Barton's sudden rise to—well, at least newspaper fame. There was no politics connected with Barton's rise. Politics had forgotten him years ago. Now the papers, the people, were forcing the mayor to act.

Why—he'd be Chief Inspector any day. But would it all be worth the price? There was the wife, the two girls; one in her senior year at college. There was—

Barton jarred erect. There was no sound of a window opening, no sound of feet upon wood nor upon the heavy carpeted floor. Just the parting of the curtains, the figure dropping soundlessly to the floor—and the man himself was in the room.

Barton was always surprised at his appearance. Not his tightly-brushed black hair, but the piercing eyes that

seemed to be the color of molten steel; or rather, steel just
before it cooled. Maybe they weren't any color at all. Maybe
it was their direct look—a penetrating look that started
far back behind the actual pupils of the eyes—which gave
them a strange appearance of heat. Fire that had not died;
fire, perhaps, that would never die.

His height! He was tall. How tall Barton couldn't guess
within—oh, quite a few inches. And he was good at sizing
up men.

Many simulated a stoop. This man did too. But it was
more a crouching-forward, an alert springing position than
a stoop. And Barton couldn't tell whether it took a few
inches off his height or added a few inches on.

For a long time the two men stared at each other. It was
Barton who spoke first.

"By God!" he said. "I ought'a know exactly who you are.
Some day I will."

Strang nodded.

"That is inevitable. But by the time you do you will have
felt the taste of power and will have to go on."

"I have felt power now," Barton said. "And I have
wondered. I was satisfied with my position as Lieutenant
of Police before you came. I was satisfied that I served the
people."

"You serve the people more now; far more."

"I wonder," Barton said. "You promised me a long talk
tonight. I'm not denying that you have made me; that you
have, far more than any other individual or set of individ-
uals, served the citizens. And I don't know if I'm thinking
more of Barton the inspector of police, or Barton the man.
But either way it would not serve a good purpose if Barton,

the man; or Barton, the servant of the city, were arrested as accessory-after-the-fact of murder."

Narrow, almost pencil-like eyebrows raised.

"Just what do you mean?"

"I mean," the inspector said slowly, "that I know you murdered

Mr. Strang

Leonard Faine today and thrust his body up in the closet. I found the picture pinned to his chest."

Strang smiled almost grotesquely.

"Nonsense, Inspector!" he said. "You joke. I killed Faine, of course; but the death of such a man is hardly murder." He threw back his coat. A dark, dull, dried red showed close to his left side. "It was self-defense. He was a very quick man with a gun. Surely you didn't miss seeing the blood in the outer hall!"

"No," said the inspector, "I didn't."

"You've come for the showdown tonight?" Strang said.

"YES. I KNOW nothing about you, except that you have a hatred for paroled convicts; at least, parole violators. You believe, and truthfully of course, that killers are turned out to prey again on society. I believe that, too. But there are several points! I gather from your hints now and then that parole violators at some time or other killed your wife—or your father."

A pause. At last the inspector was assured that he would find no answer in any sudden display of emotion.

"Anyway, someone close to you. Now, when you have met that man or men and have delivered him or them to justice, you are through. You'll drop from under."

"From under, eh?"

"Exactly!" said the inspector. "From under me."

"The man, or men, is or are dead."

"Then why this vengeance against parole violators?"

"I am afraid, Barton, you mix the word 'vengeance' with 'justice.' Those for whom I hold a personal hate were only the instruments of a greater menace. Someone close to me was killed by a 'system.' I am going to kill that system. It is called—PAROLE."

Inspector Barton looked at the man for a long time. There was nothing of insanity in those hot-steel eyes. A hate; an obsession; but not insanity. But Strang wanted to talk and Barton was willing to listen.

"I picked you in the beginning, Barton, not simply because of your views on parole. I picked you mainly because you were honest. Politics had not corrupted you; you could not be bought. You were a plugger, once you knew what to plug at, and you were without fear. I won't say that you weren't bright, but I will say that you were not brilliant. You didn't know how to fight the system and you wouldn't be sucked into it. You might some day have retired as a captain. You could and would get your man, once someone told you where that man was. I decided to tell you; to help you; to work with you against our greatest criminal terror—PAROLE."

"Against it, yes. A cop gets tired of arresting and convicting the same man over and over again. But I haven't any obsessions that a man never should regain his freedom under parole."

"Nor have I. I never have hunted the paroled convict; only the parole violator. Men who are sent straight from prison back to a life of crime; men who are freed because they are needed to commit a crime; men who are paroled because if they are not freed they will talk. I'm speaking of the professional criminal."

"Well," said the inspector, "of course the members of the parole board serve as a public duty. They can't see, interview and delve into the past and future of every prisoner. They must accept to a great extent the suggestions of the warden."

"And does the warden look personally into every case; the released convict's past and his probable future?"

"He does his best."

"Bah! And what is his best? The best a warden can do is to get his information from the assistant warden; who, if strictly honest, gets it from the guards."

"It's a question of good behavior. The guards are the logical ones to know."

"Good behavior, then, is simply the lack of bad behavior. That's what you mean! It's the old offender who knows how to work the guards. If the guards are not honest, then money jumps up a man's good marks. No, Barton. Bank robbers, stickup men, dope fiends and murderers are being turned out of our prisons every day. Some for the very simple reason that there is no more space to house them. But the greatest evil of an evil system is that parole is becoming a racket; a racket with a single man heading it.

A racket that turns men free at a price. That's the situation in this state."

3

A BULLET IN THE HEAD

"**YOU GO ALONG** the way you're going and you won't live long," Barton said. "They suspect someone, in the underworld."

"Maybe! But it's gone along pretty well so far. You have helped me, and as the commissioner of police in the greatest city of our state, you will help more." Mr. Strang turned his head slowly, looked straight at the inspector. "The *Record*, too, has influence; and it might surprise you to learn that the parole racket is controlled by just one man."

"Nonsense!" Barton said brusquely. "Such an idea is ridiculous."

Strang smiled.

"You suspect that, Barton, and I know it."

"Then who is the man?"

"I don't know."

"You mean you won't tell. It's— Steve Blake."

"No." Strang shook his head. "It is not Blake. But Blake was with Faine today when the woman was murdered. She was brutally hacked to death because she would not talk about me. And she could have talked, Barton.

"I haven't proof yet, but I think it was Blake who actually killed her. It was much more like his work. But Blake is simply an important hand of a bigger man; the man who controls things. I don't know who he is. Some day I will, and then—"

The man known simply as Mr. Strang smiled grimly.

"And then—I won't need you any more."

"You'll kill him!" Barton snapped the words. "That's it, eh?" He hesitated. He was an honest man. He wondered, was he getting too deep into the thing. Maybe he wasn't protecting a murderer, but he was protecting a killer. He knew Strang had killed Faine. He said finally:

"Strang, you are responsible for that girl's death today. She was the sole support of an invalid, widowed mother. What of that mother now?"

Strang grinned crookedly. At least, his lips curved at the left corner.

"That girl, during the time she worked for me, saved enough money to leave a fund that would support her mother in comfort as long as she lives."

"And how long did she work for you?"

"Longer than most; nearly seven months."

"Her death," said the inspector, hoping to break through the sternness of burning eyes; the hardness of that face, "was rather horrible."

"It was," Strang admitted grimly. "Very horrible indeed. But I think that she saw me enter the room before she died, and I think that she read the message in my eyes.

"Yes, it was a horrible death, Barton; but then, death to her would have been horrible anyway. She was suffering from an incurable disease; a deadly horrible disease. Another month; two, at the most. She would have quit work, gone to a hospital. The mother who loved her would have sat beside her bed for many hours; many days even, and watched her slowly die.

"It was like an insurance policy, Barton; only much more than double indemnity if she died by—well, not exactly by accident, but by violence. Yes, she looked at me, Inspector; looked at me before she died, and she knew her mother was safe; safe from the greatest fear of all humans—poverty in old age."

"So!" Inspector Barton was thinking. He was counting back. There was the disappearance of Doctor Fitzgerald just after his secretary was slain; the disappearance of the small tobacconist after the murder of his clerk. The real estate man and the lawyer too, just after the murders in their offices. In each of those murders but one the man who called himself Mr. Strang had given Barton the name of the murderer; told him where to find the man and even supplied most of the evidence. And in that one other case—a man had hung dead against the wall, much the same as the dead body of Faine had hung in the diamond broker's closet.

Barton remembered now, with a little swallow that stuck in his throat, that an autopsy on these victims of brutal death had shown each one suffering from some horrible malady. They were marked for death, not simply by the lawless who murdered them, but by the grim hand of Nature; the scourge of incurable disease.

Inspector Barton was still thinking when the man spoke. **"THAT'S RIGHT, BARTON.** I have played the part of all these men who disappeared. It was I who hired the girl who died today. You may have seen the different ads in the public notices of papers in other cities.

"Just the few simple words that a philanthropist offered free medical treatment and hospitalization to those condemned to a slow death. To many I gave such help. In some I found courage; the courage to die—die by violence that some loved one might live in comfort. You wouldn't understand, Barton. No healthy man would understand what a racked mind will suffer from a condemned body and how willing some are to die; yes, horribly, that some-one else may live in comfort."

Barton's eyes widened. He was trying to look into the future; trying to feel his way. Commissioner of Police! He saw his wife and family when his picture flashed in all newspapers. But back of it he saw other things; unpleas-ant things. His shield stripped from him, his wife and girls turned out into the street. His picture still on the front pages of the papers, but with a different caption under it. He said:

"I would like to know one thing more. Our city has a great police system. How do you, as a single individual, get and pass along to me the information that we are unable to obtain?"

"Information," Strang said slowly, "is simply a commod-ity to be purchased like any other commodity. You know murderers; you know crooks and kidnapers. There are few of them who would not betray even their own mother—at a price. One law rules the criminal. It is the law of greed. If there are times when information can not be bought for money, or the informer must involve himself too deeply, then I offer the criminal his life."

"You offer a man his life!" The inspector was puzzled. Then, "You mean, you threaten him with death?"

"Perhaps," said Mr. Strang, "I might put it better when I say that I do not take his life. I am a man with a single purpose. To wipe out the evil which is called PAROLE." And suddenly, eyes flashing brightly, "You want Steve Blake!"

The inspector's face whitened slightly. But he said:

"I want Steve Blake. The people want Steve Blake. For many crimes, that can't be hung on him."

"Would you chance sending Blake to the chair—if you could?"

"What do you mean—if I could?"

"I mean just that. Would you, even if it meant disgrace and jail for you?"

Inspector Barton straightened.

"I would, even if it meant jail for me."

Admiration shone for a moment in those burning eyes. Strang's hand shot out and clamped down on the inspector's shoulder.

"By God!" he said. "I believe you would."

"Yes," Barton's voice was low; he was thinking of his wife and the two girls, "I would."

"Good!" Strang rubbed his hands together. "It seems the thing was some years back and that you did it for a friend; a friend who betrayed you and left you holding the bag. Do you think Blake has the evidence that would remove you from the force?"

James Barton cleared his throat. His blue eyes did not avoid the burning ones. He simply said:

"You find out a great many things. The evidence against me is in a letter I wrote. Somehow Blake has obtained it from the widow of the man who had it. I make no excuses. I was wrong when I committed that act. I have tried to repay the city over and over. Yes, I think Blake has it. Quinn was in to see me today. It was just a friendly talk; but he hinted around, and I let him know that I'd take the rap before I fouled my shield again.

"They may strike at once with that letter. They may wait until they're in a big jam and think they can use me. But it doesn't matter. If I can get Blake before they strike, so much the better. How did you learn about such a letter? Why did you bring it up tonight?"

"Because," Strang said, "I am going to get that letter and return it to you."

"You—you are going to buy it from Blake?"

"WITH QUINN BEHIND him he wouldn't sell it. He holds that letter above money, but he does not hold it above his life." And when the police officer stepped toward Strang, "There! I want no thanks, I want no promise. I simply want you to believe in me; and I hope I am successful. My information comes from an agent I have trusted; one who could have divulged my identity."

Strang swung away from the outstretched hand of Barton, went to the window, stopped and turned. Then he asked the same question he always asked before he left; asked it as if he was far from sure of the answer himself. His question was simple, direct; but Inspector Barton felt that behind it was a haunting fear. He said:

"Inspector Barton; the truth now. Do you think that I am mad?"

Inspector Barton looked at him steadily, gave the answer the same careful consideration that he gave it each time it was asked. And his answer was always the same.

"No, I don't think you are mad." And then, the question he always put in return; though rather indifferently now, for he had never received an answer to it. "Why do you always ask me that?"

This time he did get an answer; an answer that jarred him back on his heels.

"I ask that because there is a bullet from a pistol imbedded in my skull at the base of my brain. Some day it will kill me; at least, eminent physicians have said so—unless I have it removed. But while the chance of a successful operation is very fair indeed, such an operation might change my whole viewpoint on life; on death too. It might tempt me to beg when I wish to force; tempt me to cure when I wish to kill. My thoughts, my acts and my single purpose must not change until my mission is completed. Good night!"

Inspector Barton didn't move for a full ten minutes after that window shut softly. Twenty-two years on the force, and he felt a tingling in his spine! He picked up the bottle of whisky, poured himself a drink, hesitated after looking at the water pitcher, then drank it straight. Barton was not a drinking man, but he didn't think of that when he repeated the dose. Then he turned and left the apartment. His steps upon the stairs were slow, methodical. Barton was a very worried man.

4

KILLERS MEET

MARTIN QUINN HAD pretentious offices! Many girls clicked away on brightly shining typewriters in the outer and main office. They were well but conservatively dressed; they had an air of breeding and refinement. All of them were not efficient workers; indeed, most of them were not. But they gave a front to the office. Martin Quinn and his friends had dealings in bonds; besides which, it was astounding the outside trade the house of Quinn actually attracted.

In his elegant private office Steve Blake rose from his desk and stood beside it as Martin Quinn looked over the books. Quinn said finally:

"That's a damn good payment to the government. They should be proud of me."

Steve Blake coughed behind a white hand, fingers neatly manicured. His voice was soft, ingratiating.

"I don't think that government tax payment there," he indicated huge figures with his fingers, "will be necessary. Indeed, it's a transaction that it would be impossible for even experts to discover."

"Mine did." Quinn nodded his head, rolls of flesh on his neck going in and out like an accordion. Then he looked up at the dapper Blake, noted the nicely-fitted blue suit so in contrast with his own loosely-fitting garments. He saw the handkerchief; blue with a white border, sticking out of his breast pocket. His lips curled slightly when he saw spats.

"My God! Blake, if I didn't know you I'd rate you a stage-door Johnny! Maybe that's best. No one would suspect you of it." Great bulging eyes rolled. "You hacked her to death, eh? And she didn't talk?"

"It was Faine," Blake said quickly.

"Oh! I know, I know." Quinn waved a hand. They've printed all that in the papers. We pulled Faine out of prison for the job, but his heart—or perhaps just his stomach wasn't in it." Quinn reached into his pocket, pulled out a roll of bills and pushed them over to Blake. "Used to be yellow, and now they're green; but they add up the same. As for that income tax business! Never fool with the government." And snapping suddenly, "Well, let's have it! Faine lost his nerve and you stepped in. Right?"

"Right!" Blake grinned. "I wanted to handle it in the first place. But you put me in the hall."

"Sure. Sure!" Quinn leaned over and patted his arm. "But you're too valuable a man, Blake. I didn't know if she knew a damn thing or not; but I thought it would give this threatening Mr. Strang a blow if the woman working for him was mussed up; make him show his hand; make him strike,"

"Make him!" Steve Blake parted great thick lips. "Didn't he? Didn't he hang Faine up like a side of beef? Why should he go haywire now?"

"Because," said Quinn sharply, "he thinks you really croaked the dame. And from the description of the lad

I had look at her in the morgue, it looks like your work. Let me have it all."

"Well"—Blake stood just a little straighter—"Faine was making a mess out of it. I was in the hall. I went in. He didn't have the guts for it. I gave it to her, Quinn; I gave it to her

Martin Quinn

good. She wouldn't or couldn't talk; half fainted before I really got started on her. But I saw it in her eyes. I gave her hell while it lasted, boss. She felt every stick, every twist, every—"

"Never mind that!" Quinn cut in. "She's dead, and this lad will know we're getting close to him. Anything else? Anything important?"

"Right!" said Blake. "Damned important. I saw this Mr. Strang."

"Hell! You did?" Quinn's huge hands rubbed together.

Blake picked up the bills, ran his fingers over them slowly, waited until Quinn dug into his pocket and fished out a roll just as large. He went through the new bunch of bills more slowly before he spoke, then he said:

"Just as thick, Quinn. But the numbers are smaller; much smaller."

"Do you think I'm a walking bank? You'll be well rewarded. Tell me about it. Who is he?"

Blake licked at his lips.

"**I SAW HIM** from the washroom. It had to be him because he was shot. Hell, it couldn't have been anyone else. You see there was blood on his hand; blood he tried to keep hidden with his handkerchief. I didn't trail him. I beat it straight for my diggings." And when Quinn scowled, "What the hell! Sirens were screeching up the street. My face is well known to the cops."

"But they have nothing on you."

"That's right!" Blake nodded. "And they ain't going to. I'll know this Strang again. I've seen him before, but I don't remember where."

"In the night life?"

"No. I think, in the papers; pictures of him. I think he's a nut, boss, just like I always did. You leaned toward the idea that he worked with Myers' crowd; but I don't think so. We've watched Myers pretty carefully. This guy is just a nut; like he writes and telephones those threats."

"Sure. Sure!" Quinn was rather doubtful. "But he makes good on his threats. Now we've got him. You better go through newspaper files this afternoon. I'll phone Potter, of the *Press*. He'll make it easy for you, without knowing what mug you're hunting for." And suddenly, "Did he see you?"

"No!" Blake was emphatic.

"Well, you better get along then; spot those files. Crazy or not crazy, this guy finds out plenty. We should put the finger on his face before night."

"We? Me!" Blake hesitated. "The big boss will like that a lot."

"Yes. I like it a lot," Quinn said.

"But I mean the lad behind; behind you, you know." Steve Blake rocked easily on the balls of his feet, but his

animal-like eyes watched Quinn. He had never gone quite
so far before.

Quinn said, turning over some papers on his desk:

"There is no other man but me."

"Yeah?" Blake tried putting his hands on the lapels of
his coat; a gun showed under his left armpit. "That's a bum
gag, boss. We all know it; all the boys."

Quinn placed the papers very carefully before him, stood
up, leaned on the desk, stuck his face very close to Blake's.
His pale blue eyes were still watery; even fish-like behind
the slight film, but there was something else behind the
film. Blake couldn't tell exactly what it was. It seemed to
him as if he looked at two sharp points. Like dots behind
ice.

"There is no one but me," Quinn said very slowly. "If
there was such an unknown person, think of his advantage
over you." Quinn's thumb went out, pounded down on the
desk. "He could snap you out like that, with no danger of
retribution. You, or even me. Understand?"

Blake felt the threat, knew it was there—and jumped
the subject.

"I'll beat it along." He picked up his hat and gloves.

"You're sure this lad, this Strang didn't see you?"

"Absolutely! I—"

Blake stopped, moved toward the ringing phone. But
Quinn lifted it, and said:

"What is it? Yes, this is Mr. Quinn. I don't see people
without… What?" A moment's wait, Quinn finally said,
"Give me a full minute, then show him right in here."

He dropped the phone down in its cradle, turned and
looked at Blake.

"So he didn't recognize you! Well, he's outside now and wants in."

Blake's right hand shot to his left armpit. His eyes bulged; he licked twice at his lips before he spoke.

"Who? Who?"

Quinn smiled.

"Don't act like a fool. The man who didn't see you, of course. Mr. Strang. Take your hand off your rod. This is a respectable office. The girls out front are all on the level. If he's our Private Enemy No. 1 or not, we can't smear him all over this office."

Blake stood speechless, then he choked out the words:

"God! It's the knife! He's got it, he knows it's mine. He must have seen me!"

Quinn was thinking half aloud and missed the beginning of Blake's choked words, or perhaps didn't get the significance of them. He only shook his head and said:

"I GUESS YOU'RE right, Blake. After those letters, those threats, after killing Faine and pegging him up in the closet—he must be mad to come here. He's playing right into our hands, or it's a trap. That's right. We'll listen and he'll talk. My cane!" Quinn reached over the desk and lifted his cane from beside it.

A knock on the door. Quinn looked quickly at Blake.

"Be ready to get at a gun if you have to. That's right; duck it to a side pocket. He may be a maniac. If he goes to shoot me, let him have it."

"Yeah. Sure!" Blake's hand moved like a flash. Something dark showed for a moment, then disappeared in his right jacket pocket. His hand stayed with it.

A prim middle-aged woman with heavy glasses opened the door when Quinn called.

The woman said, and there was doubt in her voice:

"A Mr. Strang, Mr. Quinn. I tried to explain on the phone, but—"

"That's right." Quinn nodded, jerking the cigar in his mouth up and down. "Show the gentleman in." And after a deep breath, "And don't bother to close the door." For the moment the thought flashed through his head of the Los Angeles near-tragedy, when a human bomb popped into police headquarters.

5

THE MURDER KNIFE

THE MAN CAME slowly through the doorway, each step a measured stride, as if he counted it mentally. The steel that had hardly cooled was visible in his eyes. He came up to Quinn's desk, stood before it; finally drew his hands slowly from his overcoat pocket, then spoke:

"Quite empty." He turned his hands over a couple of times. "So—quite harmless. You might close the door."

Quinn looked from those two white hands with the long, strong fingers to Blake—who gripped his gun the tighter and nodded.

"That's all, Miss Benson," Quinn said. "You may leave us alone."

The door closed softly. No one spoke; no one moved. The stranger still stood by the desk. Blake was near the window watching him. Quinn leaned back in the desk chair and spun the cane between his knees. It was Blake who couldn't stand the silence. He said, shuffling his feet, half raising his right hand to his pocket:

"Well, Mr. Strang, let's have it. You're the lad who's been buzzing the phone and writing threatening letters. Did you ever think we might hold you for blackmail?"

Quinn snapped in quickly.

"Mr. Strang's business is with me. I'll do the—"

"My business," Strang interrupted, "is with Blake. I am under the impression that he is the manager of this—this business; that your visits are rare indeed, and that the visits of another certain gentleman are so rare that I do not even know that he has been here. At least, but once—and that was in the night."

Quinn straightened more in his chair.

"We have marked you down for a crank, Mr. Strang, and you talk like a man who has brooded over a fancied grievance so long that it has now become a real one. Let me hear more about you. It is quite possible that I may not send for the police." And when Strang's hand moved to his left coat pocket, "Men in your condition of mind are sometimes dangerous. I must warn you that Mr. Blake is armed and can handle a gun."

Strang's hand dropped to his side.

"I understand that he can also handle a knife." Eyes seemed to glow even brighter, like small electric globes far back in shadows made by the pulled-down hat.

Quinn lifted the cigar from his mouth, held his cane between his knees.

"Feeling as you do, I am wondering why you came here. You have called us crooks and other things."

"Other things, yes. A new sort of racket. To get men paroled, who in return for that parole will steal, beat, kidnap, and even commit murder."

"Oh, come! Mr. Strang." Martin Quinn smiled pleasantly. "That's hardly fair. If you have read your papers closely you will see that my name is there with those other good citizens who favor a more strict system of parole. But back to your threats! If you actually believed them, you surely would not have come here without having someone waiting below. Private detectives perhaps; even the police." Quinn laughed pleasantly. "That might be it, eh?"

"There are no police downstairs. In a way I am in the same position you are. I take advantage of the police, but do not let them take advantage of me."

"I see, I see." Quinn looked over at Blake again, then toward the door marked *Private* which led to the outer hall of the office building. "We often, Mr. Strang, let visitors out that door; so it would occasion no surprise to the staff in the outer office if they did not see you again."

"Ah!" Sharp eyes brightened in the shadows. "So you're beginning to understand the real danger. And you well may! I gave the information that sent Grayer back to the pen. I rang up a police official and told him of Wallace and the kidnaped child. I gave the information to the *Record*"— he leaned forward now and glared—"yes, the information that burned Jackson to death in the electric chair only last week. Mad? Perhaps. But my final madness will come first to Blake, then to you, and last to the man who hides his face that the rats he hires may not in fear or greed betray him. I have come to give you a final warning. I want you to know."

Quinn's eyes widened. But he said:

"YOU COME TO me with such a story, such a threat, and state that there are no police downstairs, no friends waiting outside!"

Blake had passed behind Strang now, locked the door to the outer office. The white of his wrist showed above his pocket.

Mr. Strang followed Blake with his eyes.

"I told no one I was coming here; not a soul." And as Blake jerked the gun from his pocket and took a step forward, "But I think—if I cared to die now I would be quick enough to take both of you with me, despite the gun in Blake's hand. But no matter. I have found out more than I came for. You both fear me."

Blake moved nearer. His gun half raised, pointing at Strang's back. Quinn turned over a paper, spun the cane once in his hand.

"You are a brave man or a fool, Mr. Strang," he said. "You came here believing what you did of us; believing that, in our fear and hate, we would go to murder. Yet you have told no one; have no way of assuring your departure." He waved a hand toward Blake as Blake's gun raised above that slouch hat.

Strang said quickly:

"I did not say I had no way of assuring my departure. Indeed, I have." And half turning, "If Mr. Blake should bring that gun down on my head hard enough and I should remain unconscious long enough, it would cost him his life."

"What do you mean?" Blake hesitated. But his face had twisted now; his eyes had closed to twin slits. Just a gunman; a rat of the underworld. Nothing left to distinguish him now from the gutter he came from but the neatly pressed clothes.

Blake's gun swung up again; swung just as the tall man turned, put those burning eyes on the rat-like ones; looked disdainfully at the gun and said:

"I mean that the knife you used to stab the woman was not the knife you took home and no doubt very carefully cleaned. Don't sneer, Blake. And it is quite unnecessary to lie to me. I know about your knife because I have it. You left it there on the floor at the time of the murder."

"By God!" Blake's face reddened with passion, his lips quivered with hate. "You'll give it to me or—"

His gun flashed down even with his belt. His finger started to close on the trigger.

"No, Blake!" Strang spoke quietly. "In an hour from now, unless I telephone, that knife will be turned over to the police with a little description of its owner and the latest use it was put to. I'll admit the finger-prints are not as distinct as they might be, but they're good enough. I'm sure there will be no trouble in tracing the knife to you, and less trouble in establishing your presence in the building."

"Wait!" Quinn shot in. But there was no need for him to warn Blake now. The lust to kill was still in the gunman's eyes. But the passion and the hate, though not gone, were dimmed by something else. Fear was taking their place.

Quinn was speaking. His voice was soft and low. He wasn't exactly afraid; that is, afraid for himself. This was Blake's trouble. But he was afraid for the organization he had built up. Blake was a valuable man. Blake had no horror of taking human life; he just needed a pat on the back and a load of jack.

"Well, Mr. Strang, you've proved a very pretty case; a very pretty one indeed. Now, you didn't come here just to tell us of Blake's troubles." He leaned forward. "You came to make a deal."

"That's right." The man nodded. "I could have shot Blake yesterday."

"Then you didn't come for vengeance, eh?" Quinn smiled,

but his heart wasn't in the smile. "You came to offer that knife to Blake at a price; that's it, isn't it?"

"That's it." Strang nodded. "I have just discovered that Blake has something I want. No, it's not money. You offered me that long ago, on a certain phone call. I'll give up that knife for the evidence that Blake holds over a certain police inspector's head. The knife for a single letter."

"I SEE!" QUINN tightened his lips, thought for some time. Until a day ago he had believed that that letter would place much-needed influence in his hands, then he found out it wouldn't. Inspector James Barton had straightened, nodded his head, and to the hypothetical case Quinn had presented, had said:

"If I were the man you refer to I'd take the rap; daughters or no daughters, wife or no wife. The evidence you have can and most certainly will break me if I am the man. It may even send me to prison. But— one way or the other, I'll never crawl with the rats."

Quinn remembered those words now.

"I see, Strang. You intend to return this letter to a certain police inspector?"

"I intend," said Strang, "to use it as you would use it. We are alone; we may speak plainly."

"Oh! Yes. Quite plainly." Quinn chewed on the cigar, rattled the paper on the desk. "You are working with— well, the Meyers outfit, maybe? I didn't catch your answer."

"The reason is simple. I did not give any answer."

"No. But the Meyers outfit is small-time. I'll admit that they have, in a way, been a nuisance; as you have. But vermin, Mr. Strang, are not hard to clean out. It simply takes time and patience."

Strang's head jerked down.

"Correct! I have discovered that. But to other business! I believe now that you will discover my identity, but it will take you a day or two. Before that time I shall inform you when and where and just how I will return the knife for that evidence. I will get in touch directly with Mr. Blake."

Quinn tapped the desk and glared at Blake, and it was to Strang that he spoke.

"Don't you think, Mr. Strang, it would be safer to return the knife and forget that evidence now that we have met and your actual identity is only a matter of days?" And when the slouch hat moved in a decided negative, "Don't you know that Blake, beaten, his years of work against Inspector Barton taken from him, will kill you?"

"No. I know that he will not kill me."

"Why?" Quinn snapped the word.

"Because," said Strang, "Mr. Blake will be dead; very dead indeed."

Strang swung quickly, walked to the door marked *Private* and snapped back the lock.

"Good afternoon!" he said. "My visit was most delight-ful."

6

AN OFFER OF HELP

IT WAS A full two minutes before either of the men spoke in that room. Then it was Blake. His hand shot up, his gun in it. He rushed toward the hall door, gripped the knob, turned to Quinn.

"I'm not going to tell you that you'd be wasting your time, chasing him; or perhaps wasting your life," Quinn snapped. "I think you saw what I saw, Blake. You know that Mr. Strang might wait in the hall and shoot you to death."

"Hell! He isn't any great smell with me. I was thinking of the knife, of the organization, of you too, Quinn; or I'd of turned on the heat right here."

Quinn was still smiling.

"I'll have ample warning of any danger from our Mr. Strang. He explained that very thoroughly."

"What do you mean?"

"Simply—you. He sounded very much like a man who could be trusted. He said you'd die first. I'll have my warning then. This was the man you called a fool; a small-time chiseler. Well—this Strang's got murder in his heart; even down in his soul, just the same as you have. I'm warning you, Blake. I saw it plainly in his eyes. A deadly hate; the will to kill."

"He can't do anything if he wants that letter. It's a straight confession of Barton's guilt. By God, he lied! I don't believe my prints were on that knife. I don't believe Strang has it."

Every bit of loose skin on Martin Quinn's face seemed to tighten.

"You know he's got it."

"But when I lifted that knife I was sure it was mine."

"I know. This will be a lesson to you." And with a grin, "So would the electric chair have been. But I'd do you a favor any time."

"Sure. Sure!" Blake nodded. "I'll kill Strang as soon as I get that toad-sticker of mine back." Blake was pleased with the flattery of the big-time Quinn, but instinctively he had no illusions about favors. There was always a return.

"Of course. But I was thinking of Barton; of the danger to our parole racket he will be once that letter is gone. I was thinking how much brighter the future would be if he were dead," Quinn said softly.

"You—you're—" Blake swung now, looked up at Quinn. "You want me to knock off a cop; a cop like him!"

Quinn's right hand shot out, rested on Blake's shoulder. Strong fingers bit through the cloth, into the flesh.

"We won't argue, Blake. Barton must meet with a regrettable accident as soon as you have that knife back. I don't care where nor how you do it so long as it's done." Quinn paused.

"Come in," he called.

The sad-faced, middle-aged woman opened the door.

"Miss Kent is waiting. Shall she come in?"

Quinn nodded.

As the long face disappeared, Blake grabbed Quinn's arm.

"What the hell!" he said. "What about her? Why—"

"AH! MISS KENT. Close the door, please, and take a chair. That one there in the light. I'm Mr. Quinn, you know."

"Yes, I know." Miss Resa Kent crossed the room with a step that seemed slow, yet which moved her slender body with a rapidity not noticed unless one were actually watching for it or timing it.

"You know Mr. Blake, of course." Quinn watched her slip gracefully into the chair, noted the light from the window, that made black hair glisten and brown eyes mist slightly before heavy lashes lowered, protecting them from the glare. Resa Kent simply nodded to Blake, but not did speak.

Quinn went on.

"It's like this, Miss Kent." He spun the cane, stopped it by pressing quickly with the heel of his hand on the grip. "Our outer office is very particular as to the type of young ladies who adorn it. Their appearance, their demeanor, their simple, modest dress; neat to almost a primness." His bulging eyes sought her brown ones. Though his eyes were stern, a sudden admiration crept into them.

"Have I forgotten anything, Miss Kent?"

"Only their dumbness." The girl looked straight at him. "Nothing else, I think."

"Ah! Yes." Quinn smiled. "Dumbness! But you have supplied the intelligence. I mean, you must supply it if you are still desirous of working for Martin Quinn, Inc."

The girl shrugged. Finally she said:

"Go on. I won't burst out crying at the sad news."

Quinn jerked slightly. Blake scowled angrily and made faces at the girl while Quinn's back was turned. Quinn turned and read aloud from the paper in his hand:

> "Resa Kent—age twenty-two. Richmond, Va. Graduated Hallstead Academy. Financial reverses at the death of mother and father. Living with an aunt uptown.
> "Needs the position badly. If you care to break your policy of twenty-five dollars a week, you can get this one for fifteen.

"Well, you got the twenty-five. Do you know why you're here?"

"Sure!" The girl leaned languidly back in the chair. "You saw me last night at the Café Prince; and I don't know if it was your objection to my being there, my escort, or the price you tagged on my wrap when I left."

"You were with Charlie Moran. Not a good character; shall I say—not friendly to our house. Have you known him long?"

"I have known him long enough. If you mean—is he the big moment? No! But he gets around and I like to get around." She came suddenly to her feet, shot out the words. "I know what you're thinking, and it's true. My coming here was just a lie. Those girls make twenty-five per pretty easy, and they're just dumb enough to write the same letters over a dozen times without even noticing it. I got in on a pass. It can't hurt him any for me to tell now. Eddie Kapp got me in. I had a good front. But he promised to bring me inside; inside with you and Steve Blake. I know he never intended to. He was just jealous and had me in a safe spot during the days. At night—"

"Hell!" Quinn suddenly jerked the chewed cigar from his pocket and shoved it into his mouth. "I'm not interested in your nights. Kapp—Eddie Kapp! A small-time chiseler."

"Sure, sure!" Blake cut in now. "Got himself knocked over last week. She's not a bad kid, Quinn."

"You're telling me!" Quinn stared at Blake. "So you've been taking looks at her!"

"Me!" Blake thought that Quinn's bulging eyes would read the lie on his lips. "Kapp did talk to me about her, but I was busy. I spotted her once or twice and was going to talk to you about her, but something turned up. Now—"

"She's out!" Quinn glared from Blake to the girl. "Kapp was talking through his ears; things he thought he'd heard. There's no inside job in this place. If you think you've got the stuff and can get in the big money sitting some place else—why, spend the rest of the week walking around looking for that place to sit. Now"—suddenly lowering his tone—"you've been misinformed, Miss Kent."

"Okay! There are plenty other rackets." The girl made a little salute; a snappy little gesture of derision with her right hand as she started for the door.

"Just a minute, boss!" Blake cut in.

Quinn's voice grew loud. He divided his words between Blake and the girl.

"By God! Blake, that's been your trouble. A mark for a bit of dress goods. Using a boy friend like Kapp to get her in here! She speaks of a racket like it was a pink tea; talks like a movie moll. Look at that last salute; the crack wise; the pretended indifference and fake assurance! Why, I've seen the same thing in the movies a hundred times; so has she." He looked directly at her now. "Movie legs; movie tilt to her chin; movie words, that—that—"

Quinn paused. He began to see more things directly from the movies than he had thought of when he started to talk. She had a movie body, a movie grace of carriage. And he was looking at her eyes. Yes, she had a movie star's eyes too. He paused, licked his lips. You could wrap her up in ermine or sable and not be ashamed of carting that package any place.

Quinn moved forward as the girl started toward the door. His voice was soft; even low.

"WAIT A MINUTE—JUST a minute!" He stretched out a hand and laid it on her shoulder. "After all, Blake's my friend. He's spoken a good word for you." He smiled at Blake, but Blake's scowl only deepened as he saw and understood the smile on Quinn's face and the way his hand went up and patted the girl's cheek. "Of course, my dear, there would be hardly anything for you to do inside here; yet—"

His eyes turned from the girl. He looked out over the distant city. He was wondering if he was making a mistake. Women were all right; that is, they were all right with him. He knew how to handle them and he had yet to see the woman he couldn't take or leave alone. No. He'd give her the air for Blake's sake; at least, that was his thought when his eyes were off those eyes of hers; the thing in them that got him. And he couldn't understand; would never understand that it was simply the sparkle of youth. But he said abruptly:

"No. There's nothing you could do for us. Nothing."

The girl shrugged her shoulders, flung up her head.

"Maybe not. But I could tell you the real name of the man who just visited you." And smiling at two faces that, long used to controlling emotions, weren't doing so well now, "Of course I mean Mr. Strang."

"You know where he lives?" Blake's words were eager, anxious. "Where I could find him before—"

Quinn had fully recovered from his surprise. He took over the conversation, changed the words Blake might have spoken. He pinched the girl's cheeks as his teeth showed and his bulging eyes grew gentle; a soft, animal-like gentleness.

"Blake means," he said slowly, "that he is to have an appointment with Mr. Strang. He doesn't know if it will be tonight or in a day or two. But he was wondering if—"

"I know how to reach Mr. Strang," the girl cut in. "I know where he conducts his business. And I think I know where he will keep his appointment with Mr. Blake."

"Blake," said Quinn, "take Miss Kent out to lunch. Miss Kent, your information may prove very valuable."

"To both you and me." Brown eyes were steady; hard; even slightly cruel, Quinn thought.

Quinn grinned.

"One of my many faults is not—meanness," he said as he held open the private door to the outer hall.

Alone, he lifted the phone. He had to have a long talk with Senator Stone. There were certain documents out in Chicago that would be worth a fortune to him, and one man who could get inside the safe that contained them. Who would get inside—for freedom. Yes, Quinn felt that a certain Mr. Bert Lawson needed a parole.

7

THE LIGHT OF THE
DOUBLE-CROSS

CONTRARY TO THE expressed opinion of Martin Quinn, the man known as Mr. Strang did not loiter in the hall. In fact, he hurried to the street, stepped quickly into the middle of the traffic, and opening the door of a cruising taxi, was inside before the driver had come to a full stop.

His orders were not quick and sharp nor his voice one to be remembered. He gave the address to the driver, then leaned back in the cab and thought.

Mr. Strang didn't doubt that he would receive that knife. He had looked into a girl's eyes and believed her. That she would and could produce it he felt certain. Anyway, he had gone straight to Blake and Quinn on her word alone.

But he had wanted to go. His very presence in Quinn's office would convince them of the danger he held over Blake's head. Besides, they were sure to find out who he was since Blake had seen him the day of the murder. So he made the meeting of his planning and not theirs. And he had made it dramatic. Martin Quinn would look on him seriously from now on.

Yes, he was returning the knife to Blake for just one single letter. Perhaps he was letting a murderer go free that Barton should not be taken from him. But Blake's time could wait. The conviction and electrocution of one murderer meant little in his mission. And the girl had said the knife had been cleaned. Strang could not understand that; but then, he only did understand that she had Blake's knife; the real murder knife, and that she offered it to him.

At that very moment the girl he trusted was leaning across the table in a restaurant booth planning with Blake just how Mr. Strang was to die.

Strang glanced quickly up and down the street, climbed the steps of an old four-story house, and stepped inside. He went to the rear, and using his shoulder to open the swing door, entered the kitchen. He reached behind the gas range, found a circular bit of wood with a white button in the center of it, and pressed it five times.

After a moment he turned and looked at the small bell above an old clock. It buzzed softly. But the buzzing was sufficient. He came quickly to his feet, crossed the kitchen, was out on the little inclosed porch and then down the steps to the stone yard.

A large wooden fence in the rear offered little obstacle to his progress. The lifting of a board, the bending and turning of his body—and he was in the court beyond. He crossed it without breaking his stride, went directly to the back door of the building, thrust a key into a lock and was in a house on the business street. The room was far back from the street, behind a shoddy and cheap-looking pawnshop.

A thin, wizened and stooped little man stood aside for him. Simon Becker had been in business a great many years and had been before the police a great many times. But he was ignored by them lately. His misdeeds as a receiver of

stolen goods sank to insignificance before the more pretentious fences. The arrogant ward-heeler in his district had,
years before, given up all attempts to shake any real money
out of Simon Becker. His business was small; there was
nothing to excite the greed even of the petty grafters of a
great city.

Now he rubbed his hands, explained that the delay in
answering Strang's ring was caused by a customer.

"Well," said Mr. Strang, "how is business?"

SIMON BECKER STARTED to pull a long face, spread his
hands far apart in his usual deprecation, grinned, thought
better of it as he remembered the liberal attitude of his
benefactor.

"Things are not so bad; things are indeed—good. I
smoked a pipe with old Silverman last night. He is interested and will throw a bit of business my way. A big man in
the business, Mr. Strang; and he was friendly, very friendly."

"Of course. Of course!" Strang was impatient, impas-
sioned. "Now, what of Quinn, his crowd? You are beginning to attract a different clientele. What of Quinn?"

"You are always interested in Quinn. Sometimes I
wonder why."

Mr. Strang laughed.

"Because he's big, Simon. Because he confuses the police.
Because he has no single line; no single crime. He handles
everything. Everything! Don't you understand? Diamonds,
blackmail, kidnaping, safe-cracking, murder for a price.
Each one a separate and distinct trade, yet he draws them
all into one single racket and heads it.

"Heads it, yet takes no part in it; except to supply the
mechanical, political, financial, and human agencies for

the crimes. He uses none but experts in the particular line he is working on at the moment, and keeps a great many of those experts where he can find them."

"So!" Simon Becker was politely incredulous. "And where does he keep them?"

"He keeps them in the state prison and frees them on parole when he has occasion to use them."

"Always you want to find out things about these paroled men. And the answer? It never comes to me!"

"Can't you guess?" Strang grinned. "Can't you imagine what it would mean to you, and to me, behind you, if Quinn should do business with you? News quickly reaches the right parties."

"Yes, yes. It does!" Old eyes shone for a moment with greed. "Already Silverman will handle anything for me; anything too big for me to handle."

Strang stretched out a hand and laid it on the old man's shoulder.

"The day is coming, Simon, when you will pick and choose what you will handle, even from Silverman."

The old fence's chest puffed, bent shoulders grew slightly erect. For a moment his withered, parchment-like face shot forward. He saw nothing incongruous in the word "respect." Indeed, he liked it.

"Yes, yes! I understand. I'll tell you all I can learn about this Martin Quinn. Only last night Johnny Lester came to see me. There was no business done, but he is one who is growing very close to the great Martin Quinn."

Strang nodded his satisfaction.

"I must know everything about Quinn or Blake or Johnny Lester."

"I have nothing now. But Lester spoke of Quinn's great influence; and from Silverman I guessed, rather than was told, that behind Quinn is a man high in politics."

"That is the talk. That is the talk! But you have little news for me tonight." Strang walked slowly toward the door. Then he turned. His right hand closed into a fist, nails bit deeply into his palm. Rather roughly he lifted the old man's head, looked long and deeply and with a burning intensity into those faded eyes.

"Why—why do you always look at me like that?" The words were forced out of Simon Becker.

Strang's strange eyes burned, but his words were cold.

"I am looking for something in your eyes, Simon."

"What?"

"The sign of the double-cross; the fear of a rat. And the day I find that in your eyes I am going to kill you. Good night!"

8

THE TRAP IS SET

STEVE BLAKE LIKED women. He especially liked Resa
Kent; had had an eye on her for some time. Now she sat
across the table from him and calmly discussed the death
of the "terrible" Mr. Strang. Blake was feeling a bit better
about Mr. Strang now that he heard that he was simply a
crook who put greed before the law. Yes, like Quinn, Blake
had felt that Mr. Strang was an avenging angel of justice.
He couldn't quite explain it; but many of the boys took the
trip to the Big House, to the hot-seat, or just got themselves shot to death at most unexpected times.

Blake had no intention of handing a valuable letter to
Mr. Strang; that is, if he could help it. Besides, he hated
Barton. Damn that woman who wouldn't talk! And again,
damn Leonard Faine, who gagged her so she couldn't talk
before Blake went to work on her!

Blake had finished her all right. He had given the knife
a sudden angry twist. She had felt that, all right. A cry of
terrible agony had come through the gag. Well, she had
looked straight at him, seen his face; and she had to die
anyway.

Blake looked at the girl across the table, her elbows on
it, her chin sunk deep in her cupped hands, her words like

a new and catchy tune. But his thoughts were chaotic just the same; pleasantly chaotic. She was beautiful, she had promised to visit him after Mr. Strang had died. She had told him he could get the knife and keep the money. It was just that, at that moment he couldn't set his mind definitely on one of two things. The live body of the girl, or the dead body of Mr. Strang. They were both rather pleasant to contemplate.

Steve Blake jarred himself out of it. Business came first. He leaned back a bit from the table.

"Listen, beautiful. I'm no sap. But Leonard Faine made a mess of it. The police know he killed the dame and there's no harm in telling you anything I want. Of course I didn't kill her, and I didn't lose my head. Faine lost his and got killed for it.

"He was in the hall; ran suddenly in on me, slammed the door and knocked the toad-sticker from my hand. And, damn it! I must have picked up his knife, which he'd dropped near the body. Then I heard the feet in the outside hall; heard them plain enough, but never thought that it was the guy who calls himself Strang. I simply made for the other room and the private door to the hall, and told Faine to beat it by the office entrance."

"But why the separate doors?" If the girl felt any repugnance for the story of a brutal murder, it did not show in her face.

"It wouldn't do to be seen together. Just common sense."

"And the footsteps in the hall had nothing to do with it?"

"No. I didn't have any idea then that it might be danger."

"But it was, wasn't it?"

Blake shrugged his shoulders.

"There's no way to tell. I was outside the entrance and thought Faine had made the main door. Maybe this Strang came then. Maybe Faine just waited too long. I'll never know."

"No," the girl said quietly, "you'll never know." Resa Kent had a clear picture of the swaggering gangster, whom most men feared, leaning down, clutching blindly at the knife, then racing frantically from the sound of feet; feet that might be propelling Mr. Strang—who very often brought violent death.

"That's the story you told Quinn?"

"Hell, no! That's what gave me the jitters this morning. You see, Faine's knife must have looked a lot like mine. I was sure I copped up my own. But things are vague. Anyway, I took it home, cleaned it up, rubbed all the finger-prints off it. It was only later, when I looked to make sure I'd done a good cleaning job, that I realized the knife wasn't mine." His eyes squinted tightly. He didn't like to admit or even believe he had been panicky. "Whitey and Joe and some of the boys were at my apartment, and I didn't look close at first."

The girl nodded.

"It's like this, Steve. Mr. Strang is in a fair way to roast you. That letter is cheap for what you're buying. But it proves one thing: Strang's simply running a racket of his own; not tipping the police, as you and Quinn believed."

Blake ran a hand through his hair. "It certainly seems like it now." He lit a cigarette. "You don't look like a moll, Resa; you look class. You don't seem to belong."

"Thanks!" She looked straight at him. "That may help me. But I could say the same thing about you, Steve. You look like a high class business man. Smooth, educated. One used to meeting the right people."

"YEAH?" BLAKE STRAIGHTENED his tie, pushed at the handkerchief in his breast pocket. That was exactly as he pictured himself, though no one else did. "Well, maybe you're right. I wish Quinn could see it that way."

"Quinn does, but won't admit it." The girl nodded emphatically. "We'll show him you're no sap. Do just as I tell you now, and you'll have the knife, the letter, and"—she leaned far forward—"the life of Mr. Strang."

"Yeah?" Steve said again. "But you haven't told me who this Mr. Strang really is."

"I only know who he is at certain times, which may not be his real identity. But I know where he will meet you, I know where he will see you. And I know how you can kill him."

"I'm on a spot, kid; a real spot. He'll have guys search me before he sees me. He'll meet me and make the exchange in a public place. He's a killer. I saw it in his eyes."

"He'll have you searched, of course; but he'll see you alone," the girl said. "And I know where he'll see you. It's a big chair under a light. He'll sit behind a desk and look at you, and he'll make the exchange. Remember! You'll be in a big chair with a soft cushion."

She paused, looked about the dining room, then whispered, "If you push your hand down on the right side of that cushion you'll find a gun. There! Don't look like a fool, Steve. I will put it there. It'll be your own gun."

"God!" Blake nearly came to his feet. "That'll be clever; that's damned clever! Why, if he turns his head I'll just shoot him to death."

"Even if he only looks away." The girl nodded. "And you'll shoot him to death."

Doubts assailed Steve Blake. He liked to play sure things.

"Suppose he doesn't use that chair?"

"He always does."

"Suppose he should find the gun!"

"He won't," said the girl.

"But if he does find it!" Life as a rule was not very important to Steve Blake, but this was his life he was thinking of.

"You would just go through with the deal. Listen, Steve! You have to go through with it anyway—or fry. If the gun isn't there, it will be just as if I never tried to help you. You can't kill him while he holds that knife; you don't know what instructions he's given for its delivery to the police if he should die. And he won't just murder you in cold blood."

"Why not?"

Resa Kent said, in a tired voice, "You couldn't understand the reason, Steve. It isn't in you."

Steve Blake nodded. He took that as a compliment.

"Why not give me his name, or give it to Quinn?"

"To Quinn!" There was surprise in her voice. "You'll be a big guy, Steve, after this kill." And seeing the sort of hurt look in his eyes, "I mean—even bigger than Quinn; far bigger. We won't say anything to Quinn about my part in it; the gun, and all that. It'll be as if you worked the whole thing." She leaned across the table and took his hand.

"You'll like me a little then, Steve. You'll—"

"Hell!" said Steve. "You're doing this to make me like you?" He clutched her hand. "Stupid, kid! There's nothing I wouldn't do for you without—"

"Then kill this Mr. Strang, Steve." Her lips set tightly. "I want him dead."

"So. So!" Steve grinned. "So that's how it is?"

But the girl only answered:

"The gun will be in the chair. Be sure to use it."

"And how! He'll be a mess. Come on, kid, chuck another drink into yourself." Steve Blake downed a quick whisky. "Funny! I always felt you could be 'that way' about me, but I never thought you could be 'that way' about another guy. How about rolling up to my joint for a while?"

The girl shook her head.

"The dead first; the living afterwards. Remember! Not a word to Quinn. The credit belongs to you."

One hour later when Quinn buzzed him on the lunch and the girl's knowledge, Blake talked around corners. But he was a bit surprised at Quinn's keen insight.

For at parting, Quinn patted Blake on the back and said:

"If the dame's a big help and you should kill Strang, be sure to mix her up in it. Always remember, Blake, that it's better to have something on a woman than for a woman to have something on you."

"Not this one." Blake smiled confidently. "She's the nicest bit of goods that's come down the Avenue in many years."

Quinn only nodded as Blake swaggered out of his office. He had been thinking the same thing himself. He was thinking, also, that Blake was both a valuable and a dangerous man. As for the girl… Quinn had saved his money; Blake had spent his. So Quinn could throw sables and jewels and cars around in a way Blake couldn't. Sables and

diamonds and cars! Quinn nodded. He knew women. His
kind of women.

9

KNIFE AND GUN

MR. STRANG CAME into the large studio, passed down the narrow hall, turned directly to the right and entered a door which bore the gold letters—"CARTER CUMMINGS—Director." It was a fairly good-sized room, with heavy drapes, a long couch, two or three side chairs and an easy chair beneath a lamp. He nodded to the man behind the desk.

"Good evening, Maxie. Feeling fairly fit tonight?"

"Fit enough to stay here tonight with you, Strang. Blake is bad."

Mr. Strang, who had now taken on the identity of Carter Cummings, smiled.

"Don't worry, Maxie. And tonight you must leave me alone."

Maxie made no plea to stay; he knew better than that. He simply walked to the door, paused, turned.

"This room is close to the street. The building itself is very open and the studio has a great many exits."

"I chose it because of its many exits."

"But sounds; loud noises; guns—you understand. They would be heard outside."

"There will be no gun-shots; no disturbance of any kind.

I am giving a rat something he believes will save his life. He will sneak in and sneak out. You have your instructions. You will pick up Blake in the park; you will drive a block before searching him; you will not disturb, above all else, an envelope which he will carry. And you will see that he enters this room without any weapon of any kind. Then you will leave at once."

"Are you sure, boss, I better not stay around? In the hall, the street even?"

Carter Cummings' lips set rather tightly. He said, "My orders are—that you leave at once."

It was about one hour later that Mr. Carter Cummings looked up, to see the green light burning above the door. He pressed a button leisurely, opened a drawer, and taking out a heavy revolver, laid it on the desk. He said, "Come in!" almost the second the rap sounded on the door.

The girl closed the door behind her, stood a moment looking at him, then crossed the room toward the couch.

Carter Cummings pointed to the chair.

"All my visitors sit there, Miss Kent. Surely by now you understand my rules! The reason for that chair is that the distance is short enough to see my visitor plainly, and far enough away so that a single leap will not permit hands to reach my throat."

He nodded down at the gun. "You understand that my business is not one in which a man can take chances."

"That's right." Resa Kent turned. She laid a long, folded scarf down upon the polished desk. It clinked slightly. Then she moved sideways along the desk, swung quickly so that her back was to Carter Cummings when she reached the soft deep chair. In such a position he did not see the large pocketbook she carried slip open, and the soft cushion of the chair and her light cough hid the pat of the thing that dropped from her bag.

Resa Kent spun quickly and sat down. There was no expression on her face to warn the man behind the desk that beneath her was a .38 revolver. He spoke when she laid her bag flat upon her knees.

"It's a rather large bag." Carter Cummings rose, stretched out a hand and took it from her. "Just rules; not suspicion, Miss Kent." He laid the bag on the desk. "I am not going to look into it, nor do I intend to question you about your private affairs." He looked steadily at her beneath the light.

"I pride myself on reading character. There is something good and trust-inspiring and loyal in your eyes, and there is also that indefinable thing called breeding in your face. I trust you, of course. But our greatest character readers are all too often wrong." He tapped the bag. "I would not mind being wrong, but I would detest being both wrong and dead."

"You may look in it if you wish," the girl said.

"No!" Cummings shook his head. "I held it in my hand, you know, and it is not heavy enough to contain a gun."

Resa Kent's teeth showed.

"Women throw acid," she told him bluntly. "Its weight is negligible and the bottle that holds it can be very light indeed."

The man laughed. It was the first time the girl had heard him laugh; she was not sure that she liked it. He pushed the bag to one side of the desk.

"To business!" He looked straight at her. "Despite the lack of make-up you do not look ill; indeed, you look very well. You see, Miss Kent, I didn't exactly take you on. You forced yourself upon me. Your story that one of the unfortunates that visited me met you accidentally I did not believe. But you discovered this place of mine and my real name which is—Carter Cummings."

"Your real name!" There was the slightest inflection in her voice.

"WELL, MY NAME for the time being. I was seen yesterday by Steve Blake. That's why I wished this deal to go through fast." Lifting the scarf upon the desk, he unwrapped it and held a knife before him. "This is the knife that killed the woman who worked for me? Now, Miss Kent, you have always promised me big things and given me very little. You telephoned me that you had the knife; that it was Blake's knife. I believed you."

The girl smiled.

"I knew that when I saw you go right into Quinn's office. I was glad. I felt that you trusted me, then."

HE WASN'T LOOKING directly at her. He was examining the knife before he swung and put it into a drawer. He didn't see her quick, deft movements; the slightly sliding body, the sure stab of her right hand as she forced the heavy revolver down beside the cushion. He went on talking.

"Yes, somehow I trusted you. Though I would have gone anyway. But I gathered that Blake had not told the entire truth about the knife to Quinn. Will you tell it to me?"

"Yes." She sat stiffly erect. "Blake thinks he must have picked up the wrong knife after the murder, and that you picked up his knife. You should be sending him to the chair; not protecting someone else."

He looked at her sharply.

"You are giving me orders?"

"I am pointing out right and wrong. I don't know who you are protecting by giving up the knife for a letter, but I know it's someone big in political circles or the police system, and I think Blake should die."

"Yet you brought me the knife."

"Yes," she said. "I promised to work for you blindly. I do not lack loyalty."

Carter Cummings bit his lips.

"Tell me about the knife. It looks very clean and free from bloodstains, or even finger-prints."

"It is," she said. And when his eyebrows raised, "The truth is that Blake was in a panic. He reached his house with his own knife, of course. Even in a panic he did not make such a mistake; but he thinks he did, now."

"Then you got the knife from his apartment?"

"I did." She nodded vigorously. "The servants were conveniently out, for his alibi. He had two friends there. He rushed in, went straight to the bathroom, washed and cleaned the knife. The doorbell rang. He hurried back to the living room, to be with his friends if the cops came. I just slipped into the bathroom, grabbed up the knife, put another in its place; not an exact duplicate, but very close to it. Now of course, he believes he took the wrong knife home with him. He doesn't understand it; but he must believe you found it because he hasn't got it."

"How did you happen to have a duplicate?"

"Steve Blake likes quiet killings. Oh, there's never been any proof, but I have known. I knew someone was to die, because Steve talked of big money. I'd had that knife a

long time, hoping, waiting to fool him. To use it just as I
did use it."

"How did you enter his apartment?"

"I had a key to the side entrance. I entered and left that
way. It's a twelve room duplex, you know." And anticipat-
ing the question that Cummings was about to ask, "No,
he didn't give me the key. He offered to give me one, but I
didn't want him to know that I had it. The second time he
made his offer, I got an impression and had a key made. So
he can't suspect me."

"I see." Carter Cummings was not sure if he saw or not.
But he did know that he trusted the girl. Yet, trust or no
trust, his first thought was his cause… The wiping out of
the evil of parole.

"It is all very clever and rather elaborate," he said. "It
might be quite possible that you want me dead. The story
of Blake's key may not be true. He may have given it to
you, and—Blake wants me dead."

The girl's lips curled slightly.

"YOUR OWN MAN is to meet Blake. Blake will come
here unarmed. Your gun is there on the desk. Maybe I've
misjudged you, Mr. Cummings; but I came to you because
you were a man without fear. You will have a gun; Blake
will have none. Are those odds not good enough for you?"

"Yes, I guess they are." Cummings nodded, watched her.

"And you'll shoot Blake to death tonight?"

"That would be murder!"

"Is it murder when the state takes a life? Is the individual not part of the state? My God! Is that man fit to live?"

"Miss Kent," he said slowly, "you are right that he is not
fit to live. But I spoke to Blake over the phone. He has my

word that nothing will happen to him unless he causes something to happen. My word is as good with a rat as with our best citizens. And I do not go in for murder."

He hesitated a long moment, looked toward one of the pictures on the wall. "At least, any more."

"You—you fully trust me, then?" She came to her feet and he looked her slender body over carefully. It was an appraising eye, but one that missed the lure of a graceful form; the beauty of youth. He looked only for an unnatural bulge. Then he stood up, opened her coat.

The girl turned slightly red, tossed off her coat, ran her hands through the pockets, threw it over one arm. Then she extended her hand toward her bag.

Cummings took the bag, opened it, peered once quickly into it and with out explanation or even apparently noting the red in her cheeks led her to the door almost directly across from the desk.

"I am keeping my promise and letting you wait in there," he told her. "If for any reason you wish to leave, it is a slight drop from the window. The bars work easily from the inside and can be snapped back in place from the outside. You will be safe."

"And you will be perfectly safe, too," she said as the door started to close behind her. "Your trust overwhelms me."

Carter Cummings spoke sharply for the first time. And for the first time she was aware of the determination, the power, the controlled power of the man. He said:

"I was speaking simply of a personal trust. You are not dealing with a man tonight, Miss Kent. You are dealing with a mission."

For a moment just before the door groaned, closed

tightly, the girl looked into his eyes. This time she experienced a different emotion. She knew fear, the cold chill of it, far down in the pit of her stomach.

10

THE TRAP IS SPRUNG

THE DOOR CLOSED and the lock clicked behind Steve Blake. He listened as Maxie's feet beat back down the hall. He had not liked Maxie. The search had been rough; unnecessarily so.

He didn't like the arrangements in the room. He had never faced an enemy before when he didn't have a gun on him. All he had was this man's word. He hadn't understood them when Quinn and the girl had both told him Strang would keep that word.

It would be great stuff, Blake thought, if he could invite lads to his place, have them searched before they came—just on the strength of his word. Blake couldn't think of anything easier to break. The girl's promise that the rod would be there helped. But above all, he must make a good front.

Blake was the first to speak. His voice broke slightly, despite his efforts.

"I think you're getting the best of the racket, Strang," he said. And as Strang laid the knife suddenly on the desk, "So that's the toad-sticker, eh? It looks clean, damn clean."

"I washed it up for you," Strang grinned. "I didn't want a bloody knife here if the police came."

"Oh—sure." Blake felt more at ease. Slid toward the chair, saw the light above it; then without invitation abruptly dropped onto the cushions. "Sure. I'm coming clean with you. About the only thing that long-nosed friend of yours left me was the letter. I guess you pay your boys well. Here's the dirt."

Blake put his hand in his inside coat pocket, drew out an envelope and tossed it onto the desk.

"There's plenty there to park Inspector Barton up at the Big House. But he's a dumb bird. I doubt if even you can work around him."

A pause in which Blake tried desperately not to talk, but had to under the glare of hot-steel eyes, "Well, mister— why don't you say something? It's business that's got to be done. Fork over the toad-sticker." And as Strang's eyes grew harder in their burning brilliance, "They told me you were a man who meant what he said."

"You are in no danger, if that's what you mean," Strang said slowly. "And I do not talk, because I'm afraid it might work me up into shooting you down like a rat. None of that!" Strang reached out and picked up the revolver when Blake sneered.

"Don't be a fool, Blake. The temptation is very strong. That woman suffered—too much." He dropped the gun on the desk, to his right, toward Blake; picked up the envelope, dumped out the paper and read it through, comparing it with a specimen of Barton's handwriting.

Occasionally his glance shot toward the man in the chair; but he listened for his sudden jump rather than watched for it. His sudden jump! Strang could have laughed aloud at that thought, but he didn't. Blake wouldn't make a move.

He couldn't. Despite his swaggering entrance, Strang felt instinctively that inside the man was an actual fear. That impression was backed up by the little beads of perspiration that were forming on Blake's forehead.

"It looks like Barton's fist all right." Strang nodded, without looking up from the letter. "You understand Blake, that the truce is over once you leave here tonight. Many have died by your hand, but I have no proof. No, not even this time. For you left no marks upon the knife. There was nothing about it to connect you with the crime. You were, after all, just a sap, Blake."

"Yeah?" Blake's hand dug deep down in the chair and his fingers felt the cold surface of the revolver. "So you made a sap out of me, eh?"

"That's right." Strang turned his head slightly at the change in the man's voice, but saw nothing but his face—cruel and mean and hard.

"Well, maybe you did, Strang. But you should have heard that woman try to scream through the gag before she died. I stuck the knife in her, twisted it slowly and—"

"You fool! Stop!' Strang swung sharply. His hard, burning eyes were now twin points of red steel. "You're going to make me—make me—"

His right hand crept slowly toward the gun on the desk. **"DON'T TOUCH IT!"** Blake said sharply. "That's right!" he went on when he caught the change in Strang's face; the points of steel widening, sinking far back—dull, burning coals. "Yep, the woman squealed like an animal; squealed in agony even beneath the gag. I thought of you when I twisted the—*all right, reach for it if you want to!*"

Blake stretched his gun forward. He was quick with a

gun; none quicker when the other man was unarmed—and tensed to hold himself still.

Strang stared with fascination at the gun Blake had snatched from the cushions.

"Maxie!"

"Nix!" said Blake. "Maxie did his stuff. It was the dame, Resa Kent. Sure! Don't look like such a dope. She has a yen for me and planted the gun here while you looked at her pretty face. You ain't the first who picked the wrong woman and played the sap. Hand me that letter! I don't want any blood on it."

Strang didn't speak. He couldn't. He had trusted the girl. Where was his mission now? Where—

But Blake was talking.

"You give me the signal, Strang." He leaned forward, stretched out his right hand, the gun gripped tightly in steady fingers. "Just reach for the rod and I'll pop one through that thick skull of yours. Hell! You're an amateur. You like to go around pinning pretty pictures on guys' chests. Why not pin one of them on me? And you don't like my stories; you don't like to hear how the woman died. Faine hardly put a good scratch on her. I did it! I did it!"

Still frozen in his chair; still staring at Blake's gun, less than ten feet from his own head, Strang knew the truth. There were many exits to the building. The girl could have told Blake that. He straightened slightly. There was something new in Blake's eyes. He wasn't going to talk any more. Plainly Strang saw the lust to kill there, but most of all he saw it in his hand; the finger that tightened slowly—very slowly, but very surely upon the trigger of that gun.

Strang knew there wasn't a chance to live. He didn't

think about that. He knew there wasn't a chance of killing Blake, of reaching his own gun before a .38 slug hit his face. But that didn't matter. Nothing mattered. Barton would be there in a little while and see him dead—but Barton would also see him clutching a gun.

Strang threw his whole body forward onto that desk. His hand grasped his long-nosed revolver.

A roar! Burning powder in his nostrils. He jerked erect. The whole top of his head must have been blown off! He realized suddenly that he was able to think. His single thought was that his sudden forward movement had thrown Blake's aim, that the bullet had creased his head and buried itself in the wall.

His gun came up. Before he even saw Blake plainly, he saw Blake's gun. Saw it as it exploded again; exploded almost directly in his face.

His finger closed upon the trigger.

Strang did not see the mark of the bullet in Blake's face, but he followed the course of that bullet. Blake's eyes widened in surprise, his mouth dropped open. And Strang's bullet crashed into the widening gap. Surprised? Yes, the surprise seemed to remain on Blake's face; to stay in glassy, dead eyes. Blake didn't move much, just slumped there in the chair.

Strang didn't move much, either. His face was scorched, his nostrils burnt and choked with smoke. But he didn't cough; he didn't make a sound. He couldn't understand any more than Blake had understood why Blake had missed.

HINGES CREAKED. A warped door groaned, finally crashed open. Light feet beat across the room. Strang found his voice and called out huskily:

"Don't move a step further, Miss Kent. I have never shot a woman before."

Someone shouted outside on the street. The girl turned from the hall door she had just reached. She said:

"You wouldn't bring me into this now. He's dead, isn't he?" Her hand stretched toward the knob as a police whistle blew shrilly somewhere out in the night.

"Come back and stay here." Strang's hand was very steady.

"But if they discover I was here—Quinn, I mean; I can't help you any more then; any more ever."

"No," the man said slowly, "you can't help me any more—ever. It's useless to stand there and lie. Blake told me about the gun; that you planted it for him."

A door banged down the hall, glass broke, voices called.

"You couldn't shoot a woman. You—"

The girl took a step backward, toward the door, stopped, started suddenly toward him. "Oh!" she cried. "I didn't know. You've been hurt. Your face—"

She almost reached him as her hand shot into her jacket.

"Only once in a night!" Strang said bitterly. Then his right hand went up and down. His gun thudded on her forehead. She sank rather slowly to the floor. But he caught her, dragged her hand from her jacket, stared at it, then lifted her gently and carried her over to the couch. There was no knife or gun in her hand; just a handkerchief.

For a long moment he stood looking down at her. It is never pleasant to strike a woman; but neither is it pleasant to be shot or stabbed by one. He shook his head. He hadn't hit her very hard. Then he went to the desk, put the letter into his pocket and went to the door just in time to keep the police from crashing it down.

HE WAS GLAD, very glad indeed that the patrolman behind the plainclothes man knew him. Carter Cummings often came down to the studio at night, and stopped for a chat with the officer on the beat. His story now was simple and direct. He told it while the detectives grabbed the phone and talked hurriedly into it.

"The man posed as an art collector," Carter Cummings said. "Many of my clients visit me here at night. His letters of introduction were good, but—"

"You have the letters?" The detective who had left the phone lifted up the dead man's head and was looking from Blake to Cummings.

"I must have; or my secretary has. I shot him, of course. I always keep a gun here. My more expensive paintings are put in another building for the night. Vandals; thieves! You understand."

"Sure!" the detective said. "He tried to kill you and you shot him. You don't know who the man really is then, Mr.—er—"

The patrolman helped out.

"Mr. Cummings, you killed Steve Blake, and he isn't going to be missed much," the plainclothesman said. "Take it easy for a bit, Mr. Cummings. Inspector Barton is coming over."

The detective jerked a thumb at the girl just as she sat up.

"Who's the lady?" he asked.

"My secretary," Carter Cummings said, without a moment's thought or even hesitation. He didn't know why he said it; didn't have any reason. Nor was he sorry after he said it.

"That's not your mission talking now, Mr. Cummings, is it?" the girl smiled.

Detective Flannery started to turn his head and saw the trickle of blood flowing down her forehead, to drop off the end of her nose.

"In the mess too, eh? How come?"

"She was hit on the head, and—"

Cummings stopped. The girl was on her feet, fell heavily against him.

"Can't you take me home? Can't you take me away from here?" she cried softly. Then the door burst open again.

Carter Cummings swung, looked over the girl's shoulder and faced Inspector James Barton.

The cop who had first entered the room started to speak. Barton interrupted.

"Okay! I know the gentleman. Sit down, Mr. Cummings, and the young lady, too. There on the couch."

Twice the girl tried to grip Carter Cummings' hand and twice he drew it away. Inspector Barton listened to Flannery, gave a satisfied grunt when he looked into the face of the dead man, leaned over, lifted his hand. But it was a full ten minutes before he turned to Cummings and the girl.

"Come on!" he said abruptly. "I'm taking you both home."

Carter Cummings whispered:

"All danger from Blake is gone. The letter is safe."

INSPECTOR BARTON DIDN'T answer. Indeed, he didn't speak again until he sat between the girl and Cummings in the big police car on the girl.

"Where do you live?"

She gave him an address and the car swung east, went three blocks across town and stopped before a hotel. The police chauffeur opened the door. The girl bent forward, leaned half across the inspector, gripped Carter Cummings' hand.

"Good night!" she said.

Cummings did not answer; the inspector muttered gruffly. The girl crossed the sidewalk and the car sped on.

Inspector Barton turned his head, saw the burning eyes.

"So, Mr. Carter Cummings, we meet, and my greatest enemy is dead. Let me have the whole story, and it's got to be good! This looks like murder; deliberate murder. I was wondering if you did it for me."

Cummings laughed, rather low.

"I didn't kill him for you." And he told Barton the truth; all except that the girl had planted the gun in the chair. He said that the gun appeared from nowhere.

Jim Barton grunted.

"And he missed you at that distance. Steve Blake missed you! Who'll believe that? It's got to be a better story."

But that's the truth." Cummings spread his hands far apart. "Then I grabbed my gun and shot him."

"You must have been surprised." The inspector was slightly sarcastic. "And so was he, I guess."

"Yes, I guess that's true."

"Well"—Barton leaned back in the car—"you said that money could buy things. Go out and use it now. Buy yourself a doctor who will swear to taking two .38 caliber slugs out of your body. And don't look so dumb. The reason is simple. The boys will be looking for the two slugs that missed you and went into the wall and they won't find them. I'll fix the gun part. This is where I'll drop you." A sharp order to the driver and the car stopped on a dark side street near the apartment of "Mr. Strang."

"Maybe I'm dumb," Carter Cummings said vehemently. "God knows I was dumb enough tonight, but why won't those bullets be found?"

"Because," said Inspector Barton, pushing him from the car, "there were no bullets in the gun that Blake used. They were all blanks."

CARTER CUMMINGS STOOD in the darkness of the side street as the car jumped from the curb. He shook his head a couple of times, then walked slowly to the corner, found a taxi and climbed into it. A few minutes later, in his apartment on Park Avenue, he sipped the drink Maxie brought him.

The gun that Steve Blake drew from beside that cushion contained only blanks. Why? The girl planted that gun there. And he had thought she put the gun there because she wanted Blake to kill him. Good God! She had put the gun there because she wanted Blake dead; wanted to force him to kill Blake!

Carter Cummings put his hand in his pocket. The envelope with the evidence of Inspector Barton's earlier indiscretion was still there.

Many things went racing through his mind. But always the thought—would he see the girl again? The blow he had struck her was hard and vicious. Yet she had said "Good night" to him. He remembered now that her voice was low and soft.

Yes, he would meet her again. He felt certain of that. But

he wasn't at all certain which side of the fence she would
be on when they did meet.

LADY OF DEATH

Was It the Voice of a Traitor—the Woman's Voice That Whispered the Message That Sent Mr. Strang to a Rendezvous with the Most Vicious Spawn of the Parole Racket?

1

INFORMATION

MARTIN QUINN LEANED to the side of the desk and twisted the rounded head of his cane. Then he tapped lightly on the desk, looked over at the girl. His bulging blue eyes lacked expression, but the girl knew that he studied her. And she knew that he was waiting for her to talk. He always waited for others to talk when he felt superior and when he wanted to give the impression that he knew more than he did.

Resa Kent watched him for a long time. She watched the curve of thick lips; the knowing smile—perhaps more a smirk than a smile. And she smiled herself. It was a pleasant mocking smile, and her brown eyes shone with it. But she didn't speak. Quinn bit his lip.

"I wonder," he said, "if you would still smile if you knew what is in my mind?"

"I think so." The girl nodded. "Because I think I know what is in your mind. First, you think the deadly silence will break me down; start me talking, explaining things."

"Ah!" Heavy eyebrows went up as flabby skin tightened beneath his jaw. "So you have things that need explaining, eh?" And, leaning toward her, "Steve Blake's death, maybe!"

The girl moved her shoulders.

*Strang turned and
faced Johnny Lester*

"Blake was a rat," she said slowly. "His hand shook. Mr. Strang was turned the other way, and Blake held a gun in his hand. Steve was yellow. Strang picked his gun from the table and shot him through the head, shot him through the head after Steve Blake—the tough, hard, fearless Blake had two shots at him."

"You know a lot," Quinn said, looking down at the paper before him. "Yet it was in the papers that Blake went there with the purpose of robbery; that he pulled a gun on this Mr. Strang, who is in reality Strang Cummings, owner and director of the Modern Art Gallery."

Quinn paused. "Now—Miss Kent, you and I know better. We know that Mr. Strang—we'll still call him that since all his threats to me came that way—was expecting Steve Blake and that he was to return to Blake a knife that might very easily sit Blake in the electric chair. And he was to return this knife to Blake in exchange for a letter, a letter that was written by Inspector James Barton many years ago. A letter that, despite Barton's record since then, his 'glorious record' of sending parole convicts back to prison or straight to their death—would have sent Barton to that same prison, or at least have driven him from the police force in disgrace.

"Now—" a thick stubby finger came out and pointed at

"If you want to know how it works, make a wrong move, Mr. Strang"

the girl, "Strang arranged for Blake to see him. Strang had a friend pick Blake up and drive him there. Strang knew that that friend would search Blake. Yet Blake drew a gun suddenly, fired and hit Strang twice; neither wound bad enough to cripple or even stun him. Two things fishy there! If Blake was searched, where did he get that thirty-eight gun; and if he did have a chance to use it, how was it he missed killing Strang? Blake was a good shot."

THE GIRL SAID:

"I thought you knew men. Blake never faced a man like that before; never faced a real man when that man had a gun in his hand. Blake was yellow."

"So you have all the answers. Perhaps you know where Blake got the gun after being searched. I saw the gun later at headquarters, and it was his own."

"Yes, I know where he got it." The girl nodded. "He got it from the side of the chair in which he sat. The big chair under the light, where Strang receives people. It was shoved down the side by the cushion."

Quinn's voice was very soft and low. He didn't look at the girl now; just down at his desk, at a piece of paper there.

"And perhaps you know who put it there?"

"Sure!" Resa Kent smiled. "I put it there."

"Ah!" This time Quinn seemed actually surprised. "Why!" It was not directly a question, nor just a statement, nor even a demand. It was simply—surprise.

"Because," said the girl, "I wanted this Strang Cummings killed." Her chin came up and her eyes flashed. "You want Strang dead, Mr. Quinn. Oh! You may deny that, or you may tell me it's none of my business. But you and I both know that he is a dangerous man—a most dangerous man to your business."

Quinn really tapped the desk this time. The pencil was dropped and his finger beat upon the wood. Then he picked up papers and sorted them. It was necessary for Quinn to do things with his hands when he was interested, uncertain or doubtful. He was all of that now. When he looked up again his blue eyes had a gentleness to them. But the girl knew. A deceptive gentleness! She was ready for the question when it came; even anticipated it.

"You are a very bright girl, Miss Kent; almost psychic. How do you account for knowing so much about the whole thing?"

The girl smiled.

"That's a trap, eh? You know the answer and want to see if I lie about it. But I don't lie. I was there in the next room when Blake was shot to death."

"You were the girl Strang identified as his secretary to the police that night!" This time there was no semblance of a question in Quinn's voice. It was a direct statement of fact.

"That," she said slowly, "was not in the papers. But I was that girl. And that ends that, Mr. Quinn. We reach an 'impasse' there."

" 'Impasse!' " Quinn smiled. "We are a bit elegant at times, eh? Steve Blake must have enjoyed those cracks."

"My past life," said Resa Kent, "is my own. The present belongs to those for whom I work. The future is mine also."

Quinn leaned on the desk, gripped the cane, spun it slightly.

"You looked forward to a future then, and it wasn't with Steve?"

"Kapp, and then Steve." The girl leaned back. "Stepping stones, perhaps, to that future."

QUINN LOOKED THE girl over from head to foot. She noticed the look, smiled when it was on her face. She got up from the chair and walked across the room; every move-

Resa Kent

ment of her slim young body was one of poise and grace. He said:

"You were Steve's woman?"

She smiled, shook her head, sat down again.

"No." She didn't make her words dramatic, nor did she resent his suggestion. "Steve Blake was a man of promises. I've had promises all my life. I was brought up on them. I'm a C.O.D. girl now."

Quinn grinned; uneven, white teeth showed. He said briskly:

"I suppose you want to work for me now?"

"It depends on how much you want me and what's in it for me," she snapped back. "You told me once you weren't stingy. You've got brains; you've got money." She hesitated,

Mr. Strang

smiled. "You can use the brains yourself. I can use the money."

"So you'd like to work for the man with the biggest brain. The man at the top. Me!"

Her eyes knitted closely, red lips tightened.

"It is rumored there is someone above you; some powerful man who gives you orders. It seems impossible."

Quinn screwed up his face, his fishlike eyes popped even more.

"Keep on believing it is impossible. You might discover too much."

She shook her head again.

"I cannot discover too much. Knowledge is money and money is power, and power is—" She stopped and smiled.

"Well—?" he encouraged.

"Power," she said, "is more money. Everything comes from knowledge."

"That's right." Quinn came to his feet, as if the interview was ended. "Everything comes from knowledge. Even death!"

"Well," the girl demanded, "I'm not an heiress. You told me you were not stingy. Come across! I did my part even if Blake flopped. I discovered that our Mr. Strang was also Strang Cummings."

Quinn looked at her in amazement. He had never met a girl like her. She had nerve to talk to him like that. But he rather liked it. He looked straight at the girl. He said:

"Tell me about this Strang Cummings. How were you able to get into his place that night without his knowing it?"

"But he did know it." She was not quite sure if he was setting a trap for her in the way he put it or not. "You see, I worked at the art gallery, evenings, quite often; kept Strang Cummings' books, did letters for him. In a way, I was his secretary."

"Was?"

"Well—after the other night I imagine I'm through." She pouted slightly. "Though he seemed to like me a lot, and I may think up a good story for the gun being there!"

"It would have to be a hell of a good one."

"Not when a girl like I am thinks it up." She looked at him. Certainly she was a beautiful woman. Quinn moved toward her, put his hands on her shoulders.

"Yes, a man might be fool enough to believe anything you tell him." A huge arm drifted about her neck, pulled her slowly closer. "Me! I can take my women or leave them alone. I'm not promising, kid. But you'd make a good appearance any place; even lend *me* an air with you draped over my arm. Sables and cars and a penthouse!" He laughed. "I'd give you everything but trust, sweetheart."

SHE LOOKED UP at him coldly, impersonally. Studied his rolling chins, his thick lips, his popping filmy eyes, the thinning hair that was beginning to give Quinn what he considered an intellectual forehead.

His eyes were cold, hard. She did not pull away from him; she didn't need to. Quinn felt that he held a marble statue, a beautifully carved one, but cold and lifeless just the same. His hands fell to his sides.

"I put the mental above the emotional," she told him easily. "I guess I could like you, if you're big enough."

"Big enough! What do you mean?"

"It's Silverman," she said. "We're the only two in the room, so why put on a show for me? He's the big fence; the one you use. If he opened that mouth of his he could talk plenty."

"If he could talk, he wouldn't," Quinn said. "But what of it? No one has ever put the finger on Silverman. Besides, he's been around a long time." And lower, "I've strung with him for years."

The girl moved her shoulders.

"If you string with Silverman any longer, don't you know what will happen?"

"No, I don't!" Quinn said.

"Well—you'll just string with him." The gesture of her hand to her throat was unnecessary as she moved to the door. But Quinn was before her.

"Come on!" he demanded roughly.

"Let me have it all."

"You won't trust me, Martin Quinn." The eyes the girl set on him were hard brown ones. "But I'll trust you this time. I want a grand—a single grand, and here's what it buys you. The cops will raid Silverman's tonight!" She smiled triumphantly as she studied his face. "So, with all your secret police information you didn't hear that one, eh?"

"No," he said. "No!" He reached for the phone, then dropped it. "It can't be true. And if it was— Why, Silverman can destroy all records—code or otherwise."

"He can't destroy the one in his head. It was a young girl, Quinn, a very young girl. I'm not sure if it was his only murder, but you should know; you held it over his head. That's why you think he won't dare talk! But he will. He'll make a deal; he won't let them know about the murder. He'll talk about you, talk about you for his freedom. And he'll get that freedom before you can threaten to squawk on him about the murder. He'll make a deal with the D.A., grab the money he must always have handy, and burrow into the rat-hole he has ready. They'll never find him."

This time Martin Quinn did pick up the phone; the private phone, which was not connected with the outer office switchboard. When he got his number he said:

"Joe?" waited a bit, and although his voice was low, the girl could hear every word he spoke. "What's stirring?" Another wait, and "Hell—sure! Nothing about Silverman, eh? What? You did! You damn fool, there may be a lot to it. Yes—call me back."

Then turning to the girl.

"It's all baloney, sister. You pick up—"

The girl cut in.

"If you hang onto that grand a minute longer it'll be the toughest money you ever saved."

Quinn grinned, dug into his pocket, jammed a roll of bills into her hand.

"That's for making a guess, anyway." And as she ran her

fingers through the roll, "You're the first woman who ever counted my money; at least, in front of me."

She folded the money, opened her bag and put the bills in it.

"You're a century and a half short." She extended her hand, then dropped it to her side. "But you're starting right. I'm going to be worth a lot to you, Mr. Quinn. Good day!"

MARTIN QUINN STARTED to follow her, stopped. His phone was ringing. He listened; his head moved up and down. It was his private wire. Before he fully swung around the door had slammed and the girl was gone.

For some time the conversation was one-sided, Martin Quinn contributing "yes" and "no." Words that grew from soft agreement to angry disagreement. He finally said:

"If it was public property I could read it in the papers or hear it from a dozen dumb cops. Yes, I know your information has been very valuable. Keep it that way! If I hadn't buzzed you I'd never have heard. Of course you don't know where I got it! Maybe you're not even sure yet. But I am. Yes! Good-by, and keep your ears clean from now on."

Martin slammed down the phone, waited a second or two, then dialed another number.

"I don't give a damn where he is!" he said after a bit. "I've got to see Johnny Lester at once."

Then he banged up the phone. He cursed softly. He had poured a lot of money into building up Silverman, protecting him and his many business outlets, and the old fence had made a fortune through him.

He jammed a finger down on a white button. A middle aged man came in, peered through thick glasses. He was Chester Frost, the forger; one of Quinn's mistakes. Quinn had had difficulty in obtaining Frost's parole, only to find out later that his former nimble fingers were useless. The legislature should investigate the dampness of the State Prison! But Quinn only said:

"Get me the Silverman file. I want his whole record. Sam Silverman!"

Then he sat back in his chair and twirled his gold headed cane. His lips parted and he smiled. Sam Silverman had passed his allotted time of four score years and ten. His number was up!

2

THE PAROLE RACKET

INSPECTOR JAMES BARTON cautiously opened his door and let the man in. Though the night was fairly warm for that time of the year, the man wore his overcoat collar turned up and his soft hat pulled far down. He walked with the same forward stoop. Perhaps it was not exactly a stoop; rather an alert bend—as if he expected to spring at any moment. But this was the man who, for close to two years, Barton had known simply as Mr. Strang. The man who had given him all the information which sent parole violators back to prison, to the electric chair, or often straight to their death at the hands of the police.

As he preceded the man to the library Barton grinned crookedly. There were others, too, who most certainly had died by this man's gun. Not outright murder, perhaps; but outside the law just the same. Mr. Strang, a man with a single dominating purpose—To destroy the evil of Parole and those connected with it! The Parole Racket. A racket where men bought their freedom from prison, or were released for the evil ends of a vicious system of crime.

Inspector Barton locked the door and looked over at Mr. Strang who stood before the open grate, his hands behind him, his back to the freshly blazing log. Mr. Strang, who had obtained the letter which the dead Blake had held; a letter that meant disgrace and perhaps prison for Inspector Barton.

Barton was not sorry for the deed that letter would expose. But he was sorry for the letter he had once written and until a few months before thought long since destroyed.

Mr. Strang had obtained that letter but had not returned it to Inspector Barton. Why? Barton thought that he knew the answer. Strang hoped that, in his hands, it would control Barton; control him for Mr. Strang's purpose—his obsession against parole.

Barton was the first to speak.

"I have not seen you since the death of Blake. Must be two weeks now."

Mr. Strang put those burning eyes on Inspector Barton.

"It was your advice that I find a doctor who would swear to taking two bullets out of my body. I did just that; stayed in my home and tried to think things out," he said.

Barton was silent.

"Good God! Barton," Strang said, "you don't think I had that gun planted there in that chair, with the blanks in it, as a reason for shooting Blake to death?"

Barton hesitated, then:

"No, I don't think so. You were too much surprised. The girl you called your secretary might have done it. She has not been to see you, I understand."

"So you have had me watched."

"Only an occasional man, and for your own protection. If Martin Quinn knew you were to meet Blake that night, he knows now that Mr. Strang and Strang Cummings are the same person. That knowledge might mean your death. Understand, we have nothing on Martin Quinn. But you have given him the honor of being head of this Parole Racket, and I think that I agree with you."

"Not the head; not the head!" Strang said almost vehemently. "Just the active head; or more, the active hand that takes orders from the real head. You forget Robert Carson Stone." And as Barton's eyebrows went up, "Yes, I mean Senator Robert Carson Stone, the man behind the whole evil thing."

Inspector Barton's smile disappeared, he looked into the molten steel of Strang's eyes. When he spoke he was very serious.

"You have been the cause of my success, Strang; that is not even open to argument. You tell me that the information you bring me is bought like any other commodity, and I believe you. But your continued hunting of parole violators and those who make their parole possible is 'getting' you. It is becoming more than an obsession with you. By God! Strang, it's becoming a mania! Can't you see the impossibility of a man like Senator Stone being mixed up even slightly in such a series of crimes, let alone actually heading the organization that commits them?"

STRANG LOOKED AT Barton for a full fifteen seconds. Then he said:

"We'll take up the disposition of the senator later; I have other business now. You're a strange man, Barton. Steve Blake held a letter over your head, yet could not make you a party to his crooked suggestions. I got that letter from him. I have it yet."

"Yes, I know." Barton nodded. "You told me that after

the shooting. What of it?"

"It is the same weapon in my hands as it was in Blake's." And when Barton said nothing, "You have never asked me for it. Yet you knew if you refuse to take my orders I can use that letter to break you. If you take my orders,

Johnny Lester

that letter will force you into becoming Chief Inspector."

Barton shook his head.

"You don't need to use it for that. I've been notified that I'll be Chief Inspector tomorrow morning. It doesn't seem right, Mr. Strang. Maybe I have lived down the mistake that letter discloses; maybe I've lived it down by serving the people and not seeking higher office. Now, you've forced higher office on me. I don't think I want the honor." And more slowly, "I don't think I'll accept it."

"There's your wife and daughters. They'll be proud of you. You can think of them."

"I am." Barton nodded. "The girls are young and impressive, the wife is proud to keep seeing my picture in the papers. You see, if I finally become police commissioner, the blow will be that much harder for them to bear when it falls; for me too, I guess."

"But it need not fall—ever." Strang came closer now. "While you obey my orders and—"

Barton said quickly:

"I have never taken orders from anyone, Mr. Strang. Anyone outside the Department; nor inside the Department, sometimes. Your warnings, suggestions, information might have been for my good, for it pushed me higher and higher; but mainly they served the people. Letter or no letter; disgrace or no disgrace, the very first order you give that does not best serve the citizens, I'm through. Oh! I've cut corners. I've busted regulations. But I've crossed up those who'd cross the people. It's not morals with me, not honesty. I'm just made funny. If I don't think it right I can't do it."

Mr. Strang looked at the inspector a long time, then his hand slipped into a pocket. He tossed a letter to Barton, said:

"I killed a man to get that letter; I want to be sure it's the real one—and I want it back. It sounds bad; would make bad reading in court, or in the papers."

Inspector Barton opened the envelope, took out the soiled yellow paper, read it carefully.

"That's my fist all right." He nodded agreement. "And it sounds bad, but no worse than the truth. I have no excuse. He was my friend, and the other man was not fit to live. They would have electrocuted him anyway, but not before he talked. But I don't think it was that that was in my mind. It was the wise crack he made about the dead girl. No, it wasn't resisting arrest or assaulting an officer, as it is written in the police records."

His shoulders moved, his face hardened. The years slipped back for a moment. His voice was almost vicious. "I had a couple of kids of my own; just babies then, and—

and— Yes, I forgot my duty. I never felt sorry. I've seen the dead girl's face often, but never the face of the man I killed."

BARTON FOLDED THE letter, placed it in the envelope and handed it back to Strang, He smiled rather sadly.

"Don't look so surprised," he said. "I might have destroyed it, but I don't do business that way. As you say, you killed a man to get it."

Strang laughed, opened the envelope, lifted the letter from it, and shaking it open held it above the burning log in the grate. Then he let it flutter down among the flames. Barton didn't speak until the flames consumed the paper and the tiny bits of ash were carried up the chimney. Then he said:

"You shouldn't have done that, Strang. No, you shouldn't. Such a freedom might cause me at some time to arrest you for—well, even murder."

Strang shook his head.

"Just the opposite. Threats could never push you. I want only justice and your desire to do your part."

Inspector Barton started to speak, choked slightly, and turning it into a cough tried again. Then he stretched out a hand, gripped Strang's and said abruptly:

"You've never told me where you get your information."

"And I never will. But I get it from a good source. One who knows more than anyone in the underworld."

"The girl?"

Strang laughed; at least, there was that low choking sound. But he didn't bother to answer the question. He was thinking of Simon Becker, the pawnbroker and petty fence who had been in the underworld as long as the oldest cop could remember. Yes, Simon Becker had knowledge, and Mr. Strang had brains and cash. Although Becker was interested mostly in cash, the shrewd old man realized the advantage of the triple alliance—knowledge, brains and money.

Inspector Barton interrupted his thoughts.

"So you have confidence in the girl, eh?"

"Confidence!" Strang shook his head. "I don't know. I don't know, Barton, if she placed that revolver full of blanks for Steve Blake because she wanted to save my life or because—"

"Because?" Barton encouraged.

"Or because she wanted Blake dead," Strang said abruptly as he walked closer to Inspector Barton. "I've got a list of four more for you. That's why I came tonight." He took a folded sheet from his pocket; neatly typewritten legal length paper. "Every one of the four names on that list was paroled within the year. Every one of them, I believe, was used by Quinn, though there is no evidence for such a statement. However, Quinn was responsible for their freedom. One of the four is wanted for murder; it's there on the paper. Two of them for burglary; the dates, time and place all listed—and their fake alibis. The fourth is robbery with a gun. The stick-up of a grocery store in broad daylight. The papers have been panning the Department about the last man because he was recognized and known as a parole violator. The address of his hiding place is written down there."

This as Barton ran a finger over the sheet. "You must be careful in arresting him. There's a young girl of good family with him. He introduced her to dope. She can be cured."

And after a moment, "I thought very seriously of leaving him off the list to you."

BARTON LEANED FORWARD. That was the thing he feared in the man; the mania of it.

"You intended to kill him?"

Mr. Strang smiled.

"Let us rather say that I thought of attending to his case personally. Of course I must have your word that the girl is to be cured, then sent home to her parents without either public or private knowledge of her habit or of her associations. I will arrange for the treatments myself, also defray all expenses. If you find such actions contrary to your duty, you may return to me the last of those sheets."

Inspector Barton folded the paper and put it in his pocket. It was these almost simple and seemingly natural gestures of Strang that interested Barton and also gave him a certain trust in the man. Barton said:

"I promise to do my best to arrange things for the girl. That is all I can promise."

"And that," said Mr. Strang, "is quite enough. I will see you again." He walked toward the door, paused, turned.

But Barton spoke first. He knew the question Mr. Strang always asked, and he knew from the burning in those sunken eyes that Strang often doubted the answer himself. And he knew too of the bullet that was buried somewhere in the base of Strang's brain. But he answered the question before it was put.

"No, Strang," he said. "I do not think you are mad. Let me say—you are not mad yet. You are bitter. Bitter against the world; bitter against some wrong. Yes, a personal wrong! Why in God's name don't you have that bullet removed from your head?"

Strang spoke quickly. There was a strange something in his voice. If it was fear, it was the kind of fear that makes men brave.

"When I was a younger man I had only one thought— art. I didn't have the talent to use the brush, but I had more than a talent to judge after that brush was used by others. If I had no spark of genius myself, I could see that spark quickly in other artists; recognize the coming 'great' before any of our famous collectors here or abroad even suspected it. That genius I still retain; that genius has supplied the money for me to go on, for the painting I buy today is worth a fortune tomorrow; and the one I bought yesterday has sold for a fortune today. I led a reserved, yet a pleasant life." His shoulders moved. "No. That bullet taken from my head might give me the simple, pleasant thoughts I used to have, but— Don't look at me like that! God knows I long for them again, and yet I can't—I can't. Not till my work is finished."

"But you can't break up this system alone, Strang. You can't just kill these men."

"No?" Strang straightened, and there was a decided question in his single word. "I have killed others. You know that."

"But killing and murder are two different things. You can't go to murder!"

"No. No! That's it." Strang's hand unconsciously ran across his forehead; great beads of perspiration disappeared and left his head moist. "That's the trouble; the one weakness in my mission. They are not fit to live. The people

would be better off if they died. Then shrewd clever criminals, kidnapers, and even maniacal murderers would not
be turned loose to prey again on the people who pay enormous taxes to keep them in prison. But you're right, Barton.
That's my weakness; that's the thing I cannot overcome.
I cannot shoot a man to death in cold blood. I'd give my
own life to do it, to be able to do it, to be rid of that thing
inside that stops me. God! I've spent years learning how
to shoot, learning how to draw quickly, learning how to
kill. And now I can't."

"Not murder." Barton came to his feet, placed a hand
upon Strang's shoulder.

Strang shook the hand roughly off.

"Murder. Murder! Murder!!" He laughed, and his laugh
was like a sleigh on dry pavement. His face was not the
red of anger, but white—deadly white as his hands fell to
his sides, stayed there, fingers biting into the flesh of his
palms. Suddenly he said calmly:

"Rage and hate and threats of vengeance. I am at times
little better than the beasts I hunt." And with almost a plea
in his voice, "Try to understand the terrible, agonizing fear
that I live with day and night."

"Fear!" Barton's eyes opened wide. "You?"

"The fear," said Strang, and his voice was as hard now
as the steel of his eyes that had suddenly frozen to twin
points, "that I may die before my purpose is fulfilled." He
paused. Upper teeth clamped down on a lower lip. "I have
talked like a fool, Barton." He bowed in that exaggerated
manner he occasionally assumed. "Good night!"

BARTON REACHED THE front door too late. Mr. Strang
had manipulated the chain with deft quickness and

departed. Departed without Barton telling him that he was to arrest Silverman that night; Silverman, who was close to Quinn. He had intended to tell Strang—or had he? Didn't he at times resent inside of him the earlier statement of Strang that he had first picked Barton for his plugging, plodding honesty? Barton shrugged his shoulders, smiled.

Strang was right. Inspector Barton was not an imaginative man. Even now he could not believe that Senator Stone was back of this parole racket; yet Senator Stone had been instrumental in setting many dangerous men free. Barton knew that, though it came to him indirectly; and he didn't like things indirect.

Now he had information that Strang didn't have. Information of the greatest importance; information that would forever stop the activities of Martin Quinn. Inspector Barton had evidence that would send one, Sam Silverman, to prison for a long time—longer than he'd live, at his age.

Silverman! Inspector Barton knew him, of course; knew too that he moved goods. There was very little that Barton didn't know about such criminals. But he only knew it, couldn't prove it in open court to twelve men. But now evidence that would convict Silverman was in his hands.

Barton was pleased. Oh! there was nothing in that particular evidence that would put the finger directly on Martin Quinn. But he thought that he knew Silverman and that Silverman was hardly likely to possess the noble spirit that would lay down his life for his friend, or even some years of that life. No. Silverman was a shrewd man and Silverman would drive a shrewd bargain. He would want nothing short of complete freedom, and for that he would sacrifice Quinn.

And, Quinn disposed of, would end the parole racket. And the conviction of Quinn would do something else. It would take the bullet out of Mr. Strang's head. He was curious, too, to see what sort of a man both the removal of Quinn and the removal of the bullet would produce.

And then he thought of all that Mr. Strang had done for him, and leaned toward the phone on his desk. Yes, Mr. Strang was entitled to be in on the arrest of Silverman. And his hand stopped; he chuckled slightly. What was he thinking of? Strang was no more than around the corner, let alone at the penthouse apartment which Strang Cummings, director of the Modern Art Gallery, occupied.

Well, the raid wouldn't take place until twelve o'clock that night. Barton knew Silverman's habits; knew that his servants departed before that hour; that he would find Silverman alone and ready for bed. No, he didn't expect any records or valuable written information. At the same time, if there was a possibility of anything being found, he didn't wish to give the old man the opportunity to destroy it.

3

TALK OR DIE

MR. STRANG REACHED the big apartment house on the fashionable Ridgewood Drive, nodded to the doorman and walking through the lobby went directly to the automatic lifts at the rear of the long hall. He pressed a button, waited for the descending elevator, then rose in the car to the top floor.

Strang's thoughts were of the girl, Resa Kent and if or when he'd see her again, and what his attitude would be toward her. She had saved his life, of course. She could have planted a loaded gun for Blake, with real death, just as well as the one with the blanks. But, and a big BUT—did Resa Kent save his life or simply take the life of Steve Blake?

Strang left the elevator, walked across the narrow hall and mounted the steps which led to his penthouse. Still deep in thought he reached his own door. There was a little red light burning dimly just above the entrance to his apartment. He hesitated for a second, found his keys, stuck one in the lock and turned it quickly. His eyebrows raised slightly when the door opened at once with the simple twist of that key. He stepped inside, closed the door behind him, regarded the unused chain, snapped it into place and looked at it gravely.

He took off his hat and coat, hung them carefully on the costumer. He whistled a popular tune. Then still whistling, he walked down the dimly lit hall, passed between the heavy open drapes and stood for a moment in the darkness of the living room. His hand slipped along the wall, found the switch. There was a dull click and the room was flooded with light.

A man spoke almost at once.

"Don't go for a gun, Mr. Strang, unless you want to die before your time."

Strang blinked in the sudden light. But he saw the man who sat in the chair, the only chair in that room that directly faced the entrance and left the back of the man who occupied it unexposed to either window or door. Behind the man were heavy drapes, and if one bothered to look behind those drapes, there was a picture. A picture that might possibly shock the sensibilities of some timid visitors; yes, might even at times shock the sensibilities of the most vicious, the most depraved murderers.

There was no fear, no emotion, and certainly no surprise in Strang's voice.

"Die before my time! How long before my time, Mr. Johnny Lester?"

Johnny Lester half raised the gun he held so easily, almost indifferently in his hand. Strang nodded his approval. He was slightly pleased that Johnny Lester recognized his own proficiency with a gun. The gunman's laugh was not entirely natural. He said:

"Oh! About five minutes before your time. Stand just where you are."

Johnny Lester came slowly to his feet. Narrow eyes never

left the white, empty hands of Mr. Strang. He stuck the gun against Strang's stomach, ordered him to raise his hands and with his free left hand deftly went over Mr. Strang's person. He found a gun in the shoulder harness and another, a small caliber automatic, in a hip pocket. Once, when Strang moved slightly, he said:

"I don't have to talk, Mister. If you'd rather have it right now, try another fan dance."

JOHNNY LESTER'S FRISK was thorough. He tossed the two guns onto the couch.

Mr. Strang looked at those shrewd, mean eyes, the rather sharp nose, and beneath the long thick gash of a mouth, a chin that had trouble being pugnacious. Then he took in the elegant attire of Johnny Lester. Though the colors didn't match and were unpleasant to the eye of an art collector, there was no doubt of their high price.

"You've changed somewhat, Johnny," Strang said slowly. "There's quite a bit of money in my wallet and some small change in my right hand trouser pocket."

Johnny showed slightly stained teeth.

"I haven't changed any. It's just that I'm not superstitious. I don't mind searching a dead man or taking money from him."

Strang stared at the man, smiled grimly. Backed up by the force of the gun against his stomach, he dropped onto the seat of a straight-backed chair.

Johnny Lester retreated a foot or two, sat down in the same chair that he had occupied before, said:

"You're not afraid of death, Mr. Strang?"

"No!" said Strang. "That is, not when my mission is finished."

Lester's narrow eyes widened.

"Your mission is finished then?"

"No!" said Strang. And suddenly, "Nor is my life—yet. Don't you see, Lester, the impossibility of your getting away with this?"

Johnny Lester shrugged. His eyes were hard.

"No, I don't. And I know your mission. It is to send poor hard-working guys like me back to stir." He grinned crookedly. "Now, my mission is to prevent you sending any more back!"

"You saw my painting; the one behind you?" Strang said.

Johnny Lester didn't move his eyes from Strang. He said:

"The one with the curtains before it? Sure, I saw it— painting of a guy frying in the chair. It'll just make me more careful. This is a big apartment house and so many guys come in and out, if they did see me they wouldn't remember. And self-service elevators too. Once we knew you for Strang Cummings and once we located this place, you put yourself in a spot—a real spot. Grin if you want to, but it's a rub-out."

"Why?" Strang put burning eyes on Lester and the man saw something in them that made him suddenly uneasy. A mocking something that he couldn't understand; something that sent his eyes drifting about the place; to the mirror behind Strang, his ears tuned for the opening of the entrance door.

Finally, assured, he said:

"Well, for one reason—you're lining me up for a burn or a return to prison. For another reason—there's ten grand in it for me. There's a double kill for tonight, and—"

The hand that Strang had started to raise from his knee

hung a moment in the air and dropped back again. He leaned forward as he said sharply, as a man who was the master of the situation, not the victim of it.

"Who else is to die?"

THEN THE SHARPNESS went out of Strang's voice, thickness crept in. Was the other one the girl? Had Quinn suspected her part in the death of Steve Blake? "Who is the other? A—a—?" He started the word "woman"; felt it on his tongue, but it died there. He didn't dare put ideas into this man's head.

Johnny Lester moved broad shoulders.

"What do you care about the other? It's you and you only we both are interested in now. Can't you guess why I didn't kill you sooner; why I'm waiting?"

Strang said:

"Steve Blake was your pal. You want to know exactly how he died?"

Johnny Lester laughed.

"Steve Blake was my boss. Steve Blake held the job I should have had and now have got. So long as he's dead, the 'how' part don't matter. It was a nice job from my way of looking at it. But I've got other business. Now, *Mister* Strang, I don't mind telling you why I've waited so long. I'm willing to pass you up if you tell me where you get your information."

Strang leaned back and laughed. It was not a nice laugh; it grated even on the nerves of Lester. The gunman moved slightly forward. His words shot through his teeth.

"All right! I'm not a fool. I don't expect you to believe that. You believe I'll kill you anyway?"

"I believe that's why you came here and I believe you've

killed others." It was Strang who leaned forward now. "People of mine. People who worked for me. People who—"

"To hell with that!" Johnny Lester waved his gun. "Do you want it in the stomach or straight through the head? You've got to die. It's easy through the head; no pain. Guys that get it in the stomach stand up and stagger all around, then talk anyway, before they get another jolt." His gun went forward again. "Well—is it 'talk' or lead in the belly?" He paused, waiting. Strang was silent. Then: "All right, then; in the stomach!"

A further forward movement of Johnny Lester's body was stopped suddenly. He jerked erect, his eyes stared— stared wide at Strang. Johnny heard the voice that spoke behind him but he didn't need the voice. He knew the feel of the thing, round and hard and cold against the back of his neck. The voice said:

"Well, Mr. Strang, the place is safe for a kill, as Johnny says. Will I put one through the back of his head—now?"

Johnny Lester clutched his gun wildly. Of course he understood that there was a man behind him, that there was a gun against his neck, and that death was almost certain. But what he didn't understand was how the man got there; where he came from.

Then his shifty eyes caught the picture reflected in the mirror behind Mr. Strang. And he understood. The painting of the man in the death chair had gone. The curtains before it had parted, and a man with a gun stood there. A man with a face that was deadly white, a face that was dried of all blood, a mouth that twisted slightly at the corners as if in pain, whose eyes burnt dully far back in his head; but whose hand—the hand that held the gun—was steady.

MR. STRANG HALF waved a hand.

"No, no, Maxie—not yet." And to Johnny Lester, "Drop your gun to the floor, Lester."

Lester's hand shook. But fingers tightened on the gun. He fairly snarled the words.

"Not me! Not me, Strang! He can't get me before I get you."

Strang let his eyes drift slowly from Johnny Lester's gun to his eyes; the paleness of his former ruddy face, now almost yellow. When he spoke his voice was low—very calm.

"I'm afraid that's poor figuring, Lester. Dead men don't shoot, for one thing. For another—look at your hand. You'd probably miss me; certainly not give me a vital wound, even at this distance. So you can't drop the gun, Lester, and you can't shoot it."

The softness went out of Strang's voice, a hardness crept in. He came to his feet. "And do you know why you can't? It's because you won't be able to even close a finger on that trigger." Mr. Strang moved closer. "I'm going to take that gun right out of your hand, Lester."

Strang took another step forward. Two men cried out a warning, as one. Maxie's warning was low, and smothered by Lester's; which was a high pitched scream that turned into a shriek.

"No! No! By God! I'll—I'll kill you."

The flame in Strang's eyes became a deadly spurt of fire. His words came from far back in his throat.

"No, you won't shoot, Lester. You've shot others in the back and seen them fall. You have seen the way the body slumped slowly and the grotesque position it took upon the floor. Now you're afraid; afraid to die like that." His voice raised and he took another step. "You're just a rat, Johnny."

He leaned over, gripped the barrel of the gun firmly and twisted it slowly from Johnny Lester's grip, then tossed it on the couch. As Johnny half fell, half leaned forward and buried his head in his hands, Strang spoke to Maxie.

"There was no cause for alarm. It was in his mind to kill me—but it wasn't in his stomach."

"I was afraid, Mr. Strang," Maxie said, and his voice shook now. "It wasn't like the other times when men sat there; men without the reputation of Johnny Lester. Twice I was tempted to shoot him. I wondered, too, if the red light had gone on. I wondered if the hinges on the picture squeaked as I sat in that tiny space. I wondered if the trap we sprung would work; if the days of waiting for him to force an entrance would end with your death."

"You see only the mechanical in things; in men too, Maxie. You must look inside of them. Once you spoke, I was never in the slightest danger. Give me your gun."

"You're going to kill him now, after taking such a chance!"

"I took no chance, and I don't think he'll need killing." He took the gun Maxie handed him, twisted it in his hand, then swung it suddenly down in a curved motion, and up with a straight one.

Johnny Lester's deft hands parted. His chin shot up as that moving barrel drove between his hands, caught him flush on the chin and lifted him slightly from the chair.

Johnny Lester did not cry out with the sudden pain of the attack. He was too startled for that. He sat there and stared at the eyes of Mr. Strang. His own eyes grew wide with fear as he looked into their burning depth. He seemed to cringe away from their fire.

Strang didn't threaten him with death; he didn't threaten him with torture. He didn't even mention what he was going to use the revolver for when he lifted it above the livid man's head. He said simply:

"It's my turn, Johnny. Who was the other victim you intended to kill tonight?"

"I—why, I didn't intend to—"

And he got no further. Those terrible eyes and the menacing gun cut his words dead. Strang said:

"I'm not going to argue, Lester. You killed my people, brutally killed them. I can't prove it," lips came tightly together, parted again, "I don't have to prove it here tonight. Now—the name of the other victim!"

The gun shot up. Johnny Lester's mouth opened; a tongue licked at dry lips that had trouble forming words. Then the gun started to move—and stopped. Stopped just as Lester started to talk. Stopped just as heavy hammering beat upon the outer door of the apartment.

Strang hesitated, looked at Maxie:

"Why not the bell? Why the—?"

And it came again. This time the pounding jar of a shoulder against the door.

Maxie came from behind the chair, moved across the living room to the door.

4

BEHIND THE STEEL DOOR

STRANG STOOD ABOVE the cringing Lester. He thought quickly. There was the strong room. He might put Lester there until the visitors had gone. The door was lined with steel, the lock secure. Mr. Strang had used it lately to sleep in; it afforded him safety from attack. Before he was known as Strang Cummings, it was used for a different purpose. To keep others at times. Now in it there were easy chairs, many books, pictures on the walls, a desk.

Strang saw the change come over Johnny Lester's face. It was as if he did not fear the pounding on the door, as if it gave him hope. But anything would give him hope. Still, there was a crafty, shrewd expression that didn't fit in with such a faint hope.

"Get to your feet!" Strang ordered sharply.

The outer door had opened; had been pushed violently too, Strang thought as he heard the heavy chain catch. Gruff voices, authoritative voices; and then, even louder than those of the insistent visitors, the voice of Maxie, directed back down the hall for Strang to hear.

"Yes—of course I believe you are the police." Despite the tone of his voice, Maxie's Oxford accent was quite plain.

"No. I'm Maxie, sir; Mr. Strang Cummings' assistant, and I'll have to see Mr. Cummings before—"

The door jarred, the chain clanked, and Strang acted. He said simply:

"This is your lucky day, Johnny. The window's there." He pointed across to the French windows. "The little stone court is beyond, and then the gate. It will open from the inside. That is the fire exit. I have no more desire to meet the police with you than you have with me."

Johnny Lester didn't speak as he fumbled noisily at the French windows. Mr. Strang, perfectly calm, opened the windows for him and pointed out the gate just visible in the darkness. Strang closed the window when Lester was gone, and turned to face Maxie standing in the entrance to the living room. He said quickly:

"I heard; I know. You'll hide the guns, Maxie—those on the couch, and close our painting door and pull back the drapes. You're sure they're the police?"

"There isn't a doubt of it." Maxie nodded. "They seem excited and—"

A resounding clank, a groan of wood, and Strang stepped from the living room and walked slowly down the hall.

"Just a minute, gentlemen," he said. "What is all this disturbance?"

"Open that door. This is the law!" a gruff voice boomed. "Do you want us to break it in?"

"Hardly. And I doubt that you have the right to do it. This happens to be my home. If you have a search warrant or—"

"If you're Mr. Strang Cummings," the gruff voice quieted down, "you'll know us. At least, one of us; and one of us will know you. Detective Reardon is here. I'm Sergeant Joseph Cooper. We have information that someone forced his way in on you. Come to the door and take a look. You know Reardon."

STRANG HESITATED. JOHNNY Lester must be well down the fire-escape by now; back into the building and in one of the automatic lifts, perhaps. But he still stalled for time.

The gruff voice became even more conciliating. It said:

"Reardon says it sounds like your voice—er—Strang Cummings' voice. Take a look at him, Mr. Cummings. We're here to protect you."

Strang manipulated the little round peep-hole in the door. Then, "Ah, yes! I see Detective Reardon." And the unspoken thought—that he'd recognize that dumb face any place. "If you'll stand back, Sergeant, you must know that I'll have to close the door to release the chain."

There was a movement outside, the pressure left the door. Strang slipped back the chain. Three men huddled in; all had guns in their hands. Sergeant Cooper's squat stocky form was hidden by the two plain-clothes men. He was the last in the hall but the first to speak.

"That's him, eh, Reardon?" he asked.

Reardon hesitated a long moment, peered steadily at Strang, shook his head once or twice, then said without the least bit of doubt in his voice:

"That's him all right. Sure, it's him!"

"You might," Strang led the way to the library, "explain this sudden and insistent visit."

"No one here with you, eh—only him?" The sergeant pointed to Maxie. "What's his name?"

"He," said Strang, "is Maxie, my man. He takes care of things here."

"He does, eh? Looks and speaks more like a—"

Strang's smile seemed real this time as he cut in.

"Yes, I know. Like a Harvard man. But it's really Oxford, only more understandable. Everyone flatters Maxie."

Sergeant Joseph Cooper looked straight up into those eyes. He didn't see any fire there, but he felt something back in their depths. He said, slightly indignant:

"I was going to say 'just a college man; any college.'" And turning sharply, "Where's he going?" This as he saw Maxie pass them, slip on a hat and coat and go toward the door.

"He's going out," Mr. Strang said slowly. "Certainly you have no objection to that!"

Sergeant Cooper certainly didn't. He caught the arm of Reardon, that stretched toward Maxie.

"Of course not, if you vouch for the man. Where is he going?"

Strang said easily:

"I dare say to find a carpenter to fix the door—or attempt to find one. Not an easy job this time of night." And when the sergeant's face reddened, he dropped his light manner suddenly. "Might I ask why I am indebted to you for this visit? I have shown you I am quite safe. Is that all?"

"Well—" the sergeant stroked his chin, "a lad came into this apartment house. He was seen mounting the steps to your penthouse. There was an attempt on your life not so long ago. You killed a bad man then, Mr. Cummings. The man we think came in here was his friend. It's the vengeance of the underworld, you know."

STRANG CUMMINGS LOOKED at the sergeant steadily.

A single glance sufficed for the other two men; they were marked unmistakably as plain-clothes men. It was in their dress, in their uneasy pretended indifference, in their uncertainty if they should play the heavy brutal part or the careful, ingratiating one. They were men who never spoke out of turn to the wrong person. They understood one thing perfectly. They were cogs in a big political machine, and they wanted to remain at least cogs. But the sergeant was different. Behind his floundering uncertain manner was something else; something tricky. Something doubtful. The sergeant said:

"You won't mind us searching the place, eh, Mr. Cummings?"

"There is nothing—nobody here."

"But you mightn't have looked carefully enough. It's our duty to watch over you. You can't object to us going through the place. Surely you would be glad to permit that, even encourage it! It isn't every man the police take such an interest in. Inspector Barton is particular about your safety."

Strang hesitated, then shrugged his shoulders. By this time Maxie would have taken up the trail of Johnny Lester again. But Strang was slightly apprehensive when he saw the sergeant open the French windows, look along the little terrace, even climb out upon it and switch on the lights. The man was thorough anyway.

"Inspector Barton sent you here tonight?" he asked when the sergeant had returned.

"More or less, though I wouldn't say exactly that. It's more in the general routine—this visit. Reardon says there's just one room he hasn't been in." And after a pause and with a quick sharp glance upward, "It's a steel-lined door." He tapped on it.

"Is it necessary to go into that room?" Strang said. "Don't you see that you're entirely mistaken; that I'm satisfied with your inspection; grateful for your interest?"

Sergeant Cooper stroked his chin.

"I haven't any search warrant, if that's what you mean. But the police have given you plenty of attention. There's been questions about that shooting of Blake, and forces that would like to bring it all out in the open. Maybe we did sort of bust in on you, but I thought it was an attempt on your life. Tonight's little visit doesn't have to go on record if there's no reason to bring you further into the public eye, which I understand you don't fancy. But a report goes straight on the records if I leave this apartment without searching that particular room."

Strang knew that the man was watching him from the sides of those shrewd eyes. He asked:

"Why would you put your visit on the record if I didn't show you that room, yet keep it off if I did?"

Sergeant Cooper laughed.

"That's police business. I'd look fine if someone shot you to death ten minutes after I left, and nothing on the record to show why I hadn't searched that room and why you hadn't permitted me to."

Strang smiled. If it was a forced smile it was well done; certainly it was a disarming smile.

"There's valuable paintings in there," he said. "I always keep the room locked."

"You don't think we'd steal them!"

"No." Strang dug his hand in a pocket and brought out a

key. "I guess I'll tell you the truth. I've been a little nervous myself since the—the shooting of Blake. It's a safe spot to sleep nights; I use the room for that purpose now."

Detective Reardon spoke.

"Damn sensible, if you ask me. Blake was bad; he'd have bad friends."

STRANG LEANED AGAINST the wall in the hall as the three men moved to that locked door. He had known that his apartment house was covered by the police. Barton had attended to that. But would Johnny Lester have made such a clumsy entrance that the watching police would see him? There was just one thing he couldn't understand. The attempted violent entrance of Sergeant Cooper.

He heard Sergeant Cooper grunt, curse, say something about the springs on "that damn door." It was fitted with a strong spring lock. It was not an easy door for a stranger to manipulate and certainly impossible for a stranger to tamper with from the inside, once that door sprung closed.

A minute of waiting; an exclamation or two, then hurried footsteps down the hall. The sergeant was grinning. The third detective looked at Strang and winked. Reardon said nothing; looked straight ahead. The sergeant led the way to the outer door. Strang followed.

"Well," he said, "everything satisfactory?"

"Certainly. Certainly!" There was a half leer on the sergeant's lips. "I quite understand your desire for privacy. Good night!"

Strang's eyes widened, his lips set tightly. The door had closed and they were gone.

Then he heard the noise behind him, swung quickly, threw up a hand and stepped back. In the dim light he saw her—the girl with the brown eyes, the finely chiseled face—a sinister face. It was Resa Kent.

"Good God!" he gasped. "You were in that room?"

"That's right," she said quickly. "Now let me go."

Strang's hand stretched out and rested on a soft shoulder above her evening dress. He glanced down at the wrap over her arm and the bag she carried. It was large, hardly in keeping with her attire. The last time he had seen that pocket book it had contained a gun. His right hand gripped the small wrist that held the purse.

"I want to know how you came here—and why."

"I came the same as Lester came. I was ahead of him. It was not hard to get in. Now that I see you alive I understand the reason. You were very clever. You laid a trap for Johnny Lester. Is he dead?"

"I don't go in for murder."

The girl talked quickly, looked toward the door; the way to freedom, that Strang's body blocked. "I came here to save your life. I didn't expect the police to walk in on me. Now—let me go."

"I'm not so sure," said Strang, "that you didn't come here to kill me."

"I saved your life the night Blake died. You've got to admit that. He wouldn't have come unless I put the gun there. It meant much to you to get that letter. I—I— All right." She leaned against the wall. "I'll stay and die."

"And die!" Strang knew that a man should not try to understand women; most of all, such a woman as Resa Kent. He tried to figure out where she stood in this battle against the evil of parole.

"Yes." She hurried on. "I must get to Reardon. Bribe him

not to tell who I am. Don't you see? Don't you understand? Reardon saw me there that night when you killed Steve Blake. He thinks I am your secretary. Everyone thought that, believed that. But I don't want it to reach Quinn that the girl known as your secretary the night Blake died was hidden here in your apartment tonight. Can't you see? Quinn knows I was there when Blake died. He mustn't know I was hidden here tonight."

"I see," Strang said, but he didn't see; not exactly understand then.

She went on: "I'll slip Reardon a twenty to forget he saw me. More would make even the dumb cop suspect. He'll think it's an easy twenty. He'll look on it as a simple affair. I don't want him to tell his companions; especially, Sergeant Cooper."

"But Sergeant Cooper saw you there in my room."

"Yes, yes. But he never saw me before; don't know that I was there that night when Blake died. Please don't keep me any longer! I saved your life once; you owe me mine tonight."

STRANG HESITATED. IN his mind was the picture of the girl sneaking into that room when Maxie came, or perhaps when Johnny Lester came. Then the door closed and the spring lock caught. He had hoped to see her again; had hoped to talk with her. Why? Did he trust her? Certainly not. He finally said:

"Tell me just why you are in this business. Why you first came to me, wanted to help me, had Blake killed—" he smiled. "More might take too long."

The girl stepped back, jerked her wrist free, but made no move to open the bag.

"I can tell you in a few words. Then will you let me go? Don't you understand? It's my life. Quinn will kill me."

Strang nodded.

"That's a bargain. You tell me, and you can go."

She pushed by him, but he grasped her wrist and held it tightly. Fingers bit into her flesh, fastened tightly on bone. She spoke quickly, her other hand on the knob. Her brown eyes on Strang's burning ones.

"I came to work for you because I hate where you hate." She hesitated, bit her lip, looked straight into his eyes now. "And because I love where you do not love."

"I might understand the first of that, but the last is simply jargon."

"Understanding it was not in the bargain. My life depends on minutes, seconds even. Maybe it is already too late."

For a full second their eyes locked. Then the phone rang in the living room. In that second of silence it sounded loud—insistent.

Resa Kent tore her wrist free, jerked open the door and darted out into the hall. Strang did not follow her.

The phone rang again. Strang realized he was trying to give himself a reason for letting the girl go free. He smiled slightly. The smile was not pleasant.

He lifted the handpiece. The voice came over the wire. Barton said without preliminary:

"I think it's the end of Quinn. I'll call for you in half an hour. We're to make an important arrest."

"A weak link in the chain?" Strang suggested.

"A strong link that we'll make weak with evidence. Don't

ask questions. Half an hour. I thought it only right to have you in at the death."

Strang hesitated a long moment. He thought of Johnny Lester; of that second promised murder, and of Resa Kent out somewhere in the night.

"Very well," he said finally. "I'll be here waiting for you."

He dropped the instrument back in its cradle, and crossed to the French windows. A moment later he was across the terrace, to the iron gate with the spring lock, and down the steps that would take him to the floor below. He was going to see Simon Becker, the encyclopedia of crime. If anyone knew who Johnny Lester's second victim was to be, Simon Becker would.

5

GREAT MEN MEET–AND PART

OLD SAM SILVERMAN sat motionless in his chair, his hands folded across his stomach. A long stemmed pipe hung from the cracked lips that had the slightest tinge of blue in them. Though his eyes blinked, his head never nodded. It seemed stiff and strained, as if he listened. His eyes shifted to the two revolvers visible in the partly opened desk drawer close to his right side. His lips curled slightly. His eyesight was still good, those parchment covered hands could quickly grip a gun and the strong bony fingers close as quickly upon the trigger.

On a tray was a decanter of brandy. Beside it stood empty glasses. Sam Silverman was waiting for someone—and while he waited he was going over his past. The poor immigrant boy who made his way in America! He didn't use a gun those first few years; just a bit of lead pipe on a dark street. But it didn't take Silverman long to learn that it was the man who directed the work that reaped the rewards, rather than the man who did it—the man who took the chances. Now he was in the big money, the real money. The Quinn money.

Sam Silverman was waiting for Quinn to visit him that night.

He scowled slightly. There was just one blight on his successful career. He had killed before, but not as he had killed that girl. He had made a mistake there. He had thought all women the same. And when she threatened him; threatened to rat-out on him—he smiled slightly; the memory itself was not pleasant. She hadn't known his fingers could be so strong.

His conscience never troubled him about strangling a young girl. What worried him was that Quinn knew. He had appealed to Quinn in disposing of the body. His single mistake. And that had been his only crime that was not planned carefully in advance.

But he knew things about Quinn, too, so there was nothing to worry him there. Business was good for both of them. More money was coming in every day.

And now Simon Becker, to whom he had thrown bits of trade here and there, had taken some of the work and plenty of the headaches off his mind. He frowned as he thought of that. Johnny Lester had visited Becker; he knew that. And he knew, too, or thought that he knew, that some of the Quinn trade was going directly to Becker. He didn't like that.

He had complained to Quinn; tried to arrange a meeting with him, but without success. Quinn was busy lately. There was Steve Blake's death.

A nice fellow, Steve. Mention a name, slip Steve a few grand—and that name was wiped almost immediately from the calendar of the living. Too bad about Steve.

But tonight he was to see Quinn. He could not help but feel a touch of pride at that thought. Quinn had made the appointment. Quinn, who had never before visited him at his house. And Quinn was going to straighten out the matter of Johnny Lester and Simon Becker. Anyway, Quinn—the recognized leader of the city; Silverman's city, was calling on him in person.

THE BUZZER RANG. Silverman counted the rings, came slowly to his feet. Their meeting was to be very private; not a soul inside or outside the racket was to know about it. The great Quinn was coming through the basement entrance.

As Silverman passed from the kitchen to the cellar stairs his old form straightened. Two great men were to meet—meet silently and secretly in the night. Two great men who would decide the destiny of thousands.

It was a few minutes later that Sam Silverman returned with his visitor. In the presence of Martin Quinn he had difficulty in holding himself erect and keeping his hands from rubbing together and his manner from becoming ingratiating.

For Quinn moved with the mighty; with the respectable; with the political great. Silverman met his people in the darkness of a dirty warehouse, moved his stuff through underground channels. But it was Quinn who saw that those underground channels were kept clear; Quinn who controlled the political angles.

Sam Silverman knew, as well as any living man, that there could be no crime, on the large scale he worked, without politics. He made the sales, arranged the deals. East to New York, and even to London and Paris. West to San Francisco, and even across the Pacific.

Quinn was talking; talking the very moment he sat down.

"Look here, Silverman! Your complaint about Johnny using Simon Becker is simply rot."

Silverman was determined. He set his few remaining teeth tightly and spoke.

"It's not Johnny Lester. It's you—you, Mr. Quinn." And the next moment he could have bit his tongue off for the use of "Mr." But he went on doggedly. He might as well have the show-down. There were people; hundreds of people, who feared him, too.

"It's this way." Silverman ignored any name when he spoke this time. "It could mean, this business with Becker, that you are setting up Simon Becker for future use; to take my place, perhaps."

"He's a good man, isn't he?" Quinn looked squarely at Silverman. "You see, I know you use him yourself."

"And you sent Lester around to—" Sam Silverman leaned forward. There must be no misunderstanding. "Well—to see if he might replace me!"

Quinn shook his head.

"No. We heard you were giving him some of the stuff. I didn't like it. I wanted to find out what kind of a man he was. You didn't tell me, you know."

Sam Silverman's arms came far apart. "But I use hundreds of people all over the country, and even abroad. You know that."

"But none that know they are handling Quinn stuff." Quinn leaned forward now. "None who know that there is such a thing as Quinn stuff. That's right, isn't it?"

SILVERMAN SMILED.

"None that can prove there is Quinn stuff. But everyone who knows anything about it, or guesses it. A hint of your name moves things quickly. Quinn stuff is safe; Quinn stuff brings a big figure." And when Quinn frowned, "Well, that last shipment; that—" Sam Silverman hesitated. "You have received threats from this Mr. Strang?"

"So," Quinn's loose flesh below his chin tightened to a smooth stiffness, "you got threats, eh?"

"Many have gotten threats on that shipment, and somehow Mr. Strang made good."

"Simon Becker been threatened, too?" Quinn said.

"No." Silverman permitted his lips to part and the pipe to move to one corner for safety. "Becker is the forgotten man of the underworld. That's why I use him at times."

"And have you been threatened?"

"No, of course not."

Quinn nodded. He knew that Silverman lied. But he didn't show it in his face, in his manner.

"This Simon Becker—I suppose he could step into your shoes. Oh, don't get excited, Sam. I mean—if you retired."

"Retired!" Silverman's eyes opened wide in surprise. "But one never retires who works with Martin Quinn. You've said that yourself."

"You had such ideas once," Quinn said.

"That was before there was so much money to be made. And now I have your protection. No. I don't want to retire now. No one retires on Martin Quinn." His eyes furtively searched the face of Quinn—the bulging eyes. There was nothing but a friendly pleasantness behind the fishlike film of Mr. Quinn's protruding orbs.

"We're big men in our line, Sam; you and I. I don't know what I'd do without you. We've built up a partnership. Now—understand I'm not kicking about Simon Becker, but it's you I trust, and you only. Just don't use him too much."

Sam Silverman's head turned slightly, his colorless eyes rested on Quinn's bulging ones. Things had twisted suddenly, very suddenly. Sam found himself protecting Becker; putting in a word for him. Then he stopped, said:

"You object to Simon Becker?"

"Well, no." Quinn screwed up his face. "Not exactly, if you okay him. You know your stuff, Sam, and I know mine. If Becker's the one you wish to move goods, okay. But—understand, you're responsible for my stuff, and you're accountable to me. I don't want the blame to be placed on Simon Becker later if things go wrong. You're a foxy old bird, Sam." He leaned forward and dug him in the ribs. "I've never complained—never." Quinn's voice grew confidential. "But I head an organization, and sometimes I've had to dig in my own pocket when stuff hasn't brought the right figure. You've never shown me any books of any kind, Sam."

Sam smiled.

"I'm not a fool. I never keep any written accounts."

"Oh! I don't mean that," Quinn cut in quickly. "I mean—records in code, perhaps."

"There is no code that cannot be deciphered, so I have none. I know your influence has kept my house from being searched; that is, publicly. But it has been searched privately. My office has always been in the hat I wear upon my head. My books and files are neatly arranged inside the head which contains the office. I've got a memory for figures, dates, and for facts. You know that, Quinn."

QUINN LEANED BACK.

"That's right. That's the only way to handle things. Keep everything in your head. If Simon Becker knows his stuff, keep using him."

"But it was you who were using him," Silverman objected. "I was thinking that I—"

"It's settled then," said Quinn. "I furnish the stuff and the protection, if you need it. You move the goods and get the right prices. Forget it all, Silverman. Each one to his own end!"

"And you'll call Johnny Lester off?"

"Johnny Lester," said Quinn abruptly, "works for me; directly from me. I'm glad you tipped me off; but I'll 'tend to my own men, Sam; and to your entire satisfaction."

"You think he was—? No, I don't think he was double-crossing you, Quinn." And the "Mr." dropped easily now. "I never said that; never meant that." It suddenly came to Sam Silverman that Johnny Lester used to be handy with a machine gun back in Chicago, before he came on and worked for Quinn.

"No man ever double-crosses me, Sam. Just starts to, but never finishes. Let's forget it! I'm satisfied with your mental bookkeeping. You'll be satisfied with Johnny Lester, or there won't be any more Johnny." He jerked his head toward the glasses and the decanter. "We'll drink on it, Sam."

Sam Silverman came slowly out of his seat, leaned over the desk; over the open drawer with the guns in it. He saw them and was about to close the drawer but hesitated. Those guns gave him a confidence. The talk had turned suddenly. He was vaguely uneasy.

He laid his pipe carefully on the edge of the tray, lifted

the decanter, filled the two glasses, and with one in each hand turned to Quinn.

"You know," said Quinn casually, "you're quite a guy, Sam. Here in the whole city there wasn't a guy who wanted the job of knocking you over."

Silverman's colorless eyes opened wide. And he knew the truth before he saw the hand that stretched out toward him; the hand that held a forty-five caliber revolver. Sam had been in tough spots before; had faced a gun before, and he had talked his way out of it. Now his own hand didn't tremble. He looked straight at Martin Quinn.

Quinn's lips slipped back and his teeth showed. It might have been a smile. Quinn said quietly:

"You once told me, Sam: if you want a thing done well, do it yourself. No one wanted the job of bumping you. You've got the eye on them. You've got the tongue to talk them out of it."

"That's right." Sam Silverman set his lips grimly. And suddenly a paralyzing thought struck him. A thought that set both his hands shaking so that the brandy spilled from the glasses. And that thought was—that he had talked himself out of death before by threats of vengeance by the most powerful, the most feared man in that mixture of politics and crime. And now—the man he was facing, the man who was going to kill him, was the very man whose name he had always used to save his life!

AND SAM DID it. Not with the calm absence of fear of a man who had sunk hard strong bony fingers into a young girl's throat, but with the desperation of a man half mad. His body bent, his hands shot toward that desk drawer, fumbled there as the two glasses crashed into that drawer.

But he never reached those guns; never even got his hands on them. Martin Quinn closed his finger on the trigger once; a heavy slug tore into Sam's chest. It jarred him half erect, just above the chair he had risen from a minute or two before.

Quinn pressed the trigger of his gun twice more. The first shot stopped Silverman's forward lunge; the second followed the first into his chest, pounded him hard back into the chair.

Silverman's eyes were glassy, wandering, turning balls of ice. He clawed at his chest with weak hands. Then both his hands fell on the arms of his chair. His colorless eyes still stared at Quinn. There was still consciousness in them.

Quinn looked straight at Silverman; looked into the desk drawer, lifted an empty glass and poured himself a drink of brandy. He sipped it slowly as he looked around the room, covering the floors carefully; sizing up the entire outlook much as a keen detective would after the scene of a crime. He said:

"You're a very lucky stiff, Silverman." Martin Quinn raised the glass as if to drink a toast, dropped his glance from that blood-stained chest to the tiny trickle of blood that showed on the whiteness of the sock on Silverman's left foot; down to the darker stain that was mingling with the color of the rug, forming a little pool on the floor. He stepped back a bit, raised the glass again.

"Yes, Sam. You'll go out in style; on the top of the heap. It'll be a big send-off. A week from now, death would find you hated and despised; a rat who had squealed." He could see a light of understanding in the dying man's eyes. He continued: "The cops are coming for you tonight. Someone sold you out. They've got the goods on you, and you'd talk about me."

Quinn bent forward now, without moving his feet. "You can still hear me, eh? It's a good lesson to youth, Sam. We've got to lead a good life; leave nothing in the past to reflect on us later. I looked over your record today. I was thinking of taking a chance on you. But twenty-seven years ago you ratted out on a friend; a guy who burned. Ratted out on him, Sam, to save yourself a six months' jolt."

Old Silverman was gasping now, his chest was heaving. His tongue had ceased to move frantically up and down. His head, that he had held erect so long, was leaning against the back of his chair.

Martin Quinn finished the brandy, set the glass down on the table. He drew a handkerchief from a breast packet, and laying his own gun on the desk carefully wiped the glass and the neck of the decanter. Then coolly lifting his gun again he turned to Sam Silverman.

"Nice little place. No sound will reach the street." He raised the gun, pointed it straight at Silverman's forehead. Silverman saw and understood, for the points of his eyes seemed to cross as they focused on the nose of that gun.

"You're in a bad way, Sam; a very bad way. Offhand, I'd say it was a question of minutes. But modern surgery is a great thing. Thanks for the tip about Simon Becker. He's such a good man you feared his taking the trade! Goodby, Sam. I rather admired you, but business is business."

Martin Quinn closed his finger once more on that trigger. It was not a tiny hole that appeared in Silverman's forehead. But Quinn didn't notice that. He stood there as Sam slumped down in the chair; stood there as Sam slid off that chair, twisted his body and hunched up in a heap upon the floor.

Martin Quinn took a deep breath, looked once at the decanter of brandy. Then he looked at the clock upon the mantel and, turning, walked across the room toward the door. With a single motion he swept up his coat, hat and stick. With a little smile he made sure that his gloves were in his pocket, and after one quick glance that took in the whole room he opened the door, then closed it softly behind him.

6

―

LADY OF DEATH

SIMON BECKER SAT very quietly in his chair, rubbing his hands together. Unlike Silverman, that habit had stuck to Becker over the years. Though he had never seen the inside of a prison except for short periods some years back, Becker was beginning to believe the old slogan—crime does not pay. At least, it had not paid him; not in dollars and cents—for Simon took the slogan literally. He had no sense of values, moral or material, that were not figured in dollars and cents. "Pay" meant cash and nothing else. His creed was greed.

"I am sorry, Mr. Strang." Becker tried to look steadily at those burning eyes as he repeated the same thing in a different way for the third or fourth time. "But I have heard nothing of an unexpected death tonight; certainly not of a big one." He shook his head. "I can't believe one is intended. Somehow we know—I know. I have heard nothing."

Pausing a moment he watched Mr. Strang's face. "I cannot even guess at a possible victim tonight."

Strang nodded. He knew of that quick sweep of apprehension that was carried on invisible wires, by inaudible sounds, and was felt through the underworld when someone of importance was to die. But if it was the girl, Resa Kent, no one in the underworld would know; no one would suspect.

Strang got up to leave.

"Just a moment." Simon plucked at his arm, "All that you have promised me; all that I have hoped for is about to happen, maybe. Is it you who have thrown it my way?"

"I have not time tonight to listen—only to question, and to warn you again. Never mention my name to anyone."

"But this is important." Simon Becker's voice rang with excitement; an excitement he had not known in years. "It's about Quinn and his business—here with me."

Mr. Strang swung. His eyes blazed. His own words choked out.

"Quinn. Martin Quinn! He was here in your shop?"

"No, no. Not him." Simon Becker hurried on. "But Johnny Lester was here. And he hinted—more than hinted."

"He's been here before." Strang's voice cleared.

"Yes. But it was different this time. He talked of Quinn; of his enormous business."

Strang placed a hand on Becker's shoulder, held it there.

"That's right. Some day you will get the Quinn business; all of it. I am attending to that. Good night!"

Strang passed up the stairs, across the court to the house behind, and so to the street. He looked up and down carefully.

BARTON'S CAR WAS drawing up to the front of his apartment just as Strang reached it. There was a driver in the front; Barton sat alone in the back. He swung open the door and motioned Strang in beside him.

"Going alone, eh? It's that easy?" Strang asked.

"Not exactly." Barton jerked a thumb back at a car that was following slowly half a block behind. "Got a few of the boys."

"Going to roar up with sirens screeching?"

"No," Barton smiled. "I was on the police force long before the movies started that vogue. And never mind the lad we're taking in. It'll be a big surprise to you."

Strang said abruptly:

"Tell me something about Sergeant Cooper." And he told Barton of Cooper's entrance, of Johnny Lester being at the house, of the girl, too—almost everything that had happened.

Barton looked out of the window.

"I'll look into it, Strang; look well into it. You're right. Sergeant Cooper had no orders from me. But the fact that he had Reardon and another man with him makes it look all right. From the girl's action, he wasn't tipped off by her that you were in danger. And certainly he wasn't tipped off by Johnny Lester."

"Wasn't he?" Strang tried to peer at that suddenly set and troubled face in the darkness of the closed car. "You know, Barton, I think it was Johnny Lester who tipped Sergeant Cooper off; tipped him off to come up in a certain time if things went wrong."

"Went wrong!"

"Yes. If I suddenly turned the tables on Johnny and it was his life and not mine that might be in danger. The bringing of Reardon and the other cop might have been just scenery. If Sergeant Cooper were to find me dead, he wanted witnesses. If he were to find Johnny Lester before he died, he'd have to act quickly."

"You intended to kill Lester then?"

Strang said: "I'm trying to think as Sergeant Cooper might have thought. But you know him and I don't."

"That's it," said Barton. "I know him. I don't like him. I can't judge him by what you tell me. He might have had many good reasons for coming, and it wasn't his business to inform you just how he happened to come. Cops have their stoolies; their secrets. You have yours. I don't like Cooper because he was one of those 'dollar a barrel' men on beer coming in and going out of places in the pre-Repeal days. But many a copper called it honest graft. It was the spirit of the day."

"Quinn was in liquor then, wasn't he?"

"Quinn was in everything. He's always been first in and first out of every racket. I understand he turned over his booze business for a fortune before the best of them even saw the handwriting of Repeal."

"Has Cooper got any money?" Strang asked abruptly.

"Well—he's built up a tidy sum, I guess. Not too much."

"You've looked into him before then."

"Yes, I have." Barton was emphatic. And suddenly, "What's strange about that? There are crooked cops, of course. But average them up with any other body of men— doctors, lawyers, bankers, our most respected citizens, and you'll be surprised at the result. I don't like Cooper, but I don't believe he's that crooked."

"ABOUT MAXIE!" AND as he mentioned that name the frown left Barton's face. In the few times he had seen Maxie he liked him. "Maxie always put the exact amount of whisky in my water, Strang; never too much; never too little, at the times I waited for you. Is he—"Barton paused.

"You mean—is he close to death?" Strang's burning eyes showed plainly in the darkness. "Maxie is failing fast. He is anxious to die—die by violence, in my service."

"I understand." Barton nodded. "You are the only company who will insure him. You arranged a trust fund for his family, didn't you?"

Strang nodded. "He has a wife and child in London." He smiled grimly. "Peculiar, the way our minds run. Maxie is afraid that he will live to die a natural death. I would take care of his people anyway, but that is not his way. To him, a bargain is a bargain."

"And the girl!" said Barton suddenly. "Resa Kent. Oh! I know her name, Strang. She wasn't hard to locate. She has even called on Quinn and is seen often in the night life. In fact, she gets around. How is her health?"

Strang smiled. "I would say—perfect. But please don't interfere with any of her activities yet."

Barton grinned. "Not for a million dollars," he said.

Once again those burning eyes fastened on Barton, trying to study him in the darkness. The car stopped. Strang jumped erect on the edge of the seat.

"Good God!" he gasped. "It's Silverman's place. You can't arrest him, Barton; you can't possibly do that. It would—" He stopped. He couldn't tell Barton about Simon Becker, and that it was through Silverman he wished to push Simon into Quinn's confidence.

Barton broke in.

"We can and we will arrest Sam Silverman. And we can

convict him. I have concrete evidence that will stand up in court, against Silverman."

"But that doesn't get Quinn, or Senator Stone."

"No?" There was a decided question in Barton's voice. "The evidence just reaches out and grips Sam Silverman. There is a gap, then, between Silverman and Quinn. A gap that only Silverman can fill. And he will fill it—to save his own hide. I think when I make him an offer of freedom, he will talk—talk about Martin Quinn."

"And where did you get this evidence against Silverman?"

Barton smiled.

"You'd be surprised, Strang, or maybe you wouldn't. It was a voice over the phone that directed me to some of it, and sent me some of it directly.

"It was a woman, Strang. You can guess who it might be."

STRANG DIDN'T HAVE a chance to question Barton further. The men in the other car had now surrounded the house. He and Barton followed, saw the axes raised and heard the heavy wooden door splintering just before it crashed in. Barton and Strang entered the house.

The room was full of men. Bright lights beat down on the dead body of Sam Silverman.

Dr. Farrington, the medical examiner, was kneeling over the body. A fingerprint man was already at work.

Barton watched the kneeling doctor.

DR. FARRINGTON CAME slowly to his feet. His head cocked to one side, like a bird's. He started packing his little bag, finally said:

"There is no chance of my losing my job through lack of work. Certainly the cadavers are supplied me with great regularity. Your department should run a medical school, Inspector. Plenty of material for the boys."

"What's your verdict, Doctor?" asked Barton.

"Well—" Dr. Farrington rubbed at his chin," this is not entirely official." He looked down at the bare chest with the holes in it; the single hole in the forehead. "I'd hazard a guess that Mr. Silverman had a dizzy spell and fell off the chair."

"Yeah, I can see that." Barton laughed. "What I want to know is—when he got this dizzy spell."

The doctor pulled on his gloves; snapped his bag shut.

"I would say a very few minutes before you arrived— positively within the past hour."

As the doctor turned to go, Strang stopped him.

"Could he have been killed before eleven o'clock?" he asked.

"No!" said Dr. Farrington, and his voice was emphatic. "He could not."

Strang looked at Barton when he spoke. His voice did not carry any further than the inspector's ear. He hardly more than breathed the words.

"Johnny Lester! The second murder!" And there was relief in his voice rather than horror. "Could Lester—could Quinn have discovered your plan to arrest Silverman, and killed him before he could talk?"

"No!" said Inspector Barton. "It couldn't have leaked out."

"But others knew."

"Others in the Department, yes. Others that I would have trusted with my own life."

Strang took the inspector aside now. "Was Sergeant Joseph Cooper one of those others that you trusted?"

"Of course not!" the inspector snapped.

"Could he have known?"

"Emphatically, no." And after a moment, "He could not have got it through my department."

Barton was thinking rapidly, trying to piece things together.

Strang followed Inspector Barton to the hall.

"There was no one who might have tipped him off?"

"No!" said Barton. "Except, of course, the one who gave me the evidence that would convict Sam Silverman."

"But why would he give it to Cooper?"

"I didn't say 'he.'" Barton looked closely at Strang. "I told you a woman tipped me over the phone. I'll make it clear. I'm speaking of Resa Kent. She gave me the evidence about Silverman."

Strang's hands came wide apart.

"But why should she give you the evidence that would convict Silverman, and then tell someone else that you had it?"

Barton shook his head.

"I haven't got any answer to that question." He paused, pulled at his chin. "I don't even know she gave Cooper any information. It's only a guess. But she wanted Blake dead, and you killed him. Maybe she wanted Silverman dead, too. There is little doubt that Silverman was killed because someone feared he would talk."

"But what could he say about the girl?"

"At a time like this, you ask me riddles! I don't know." And suddenly, "What could Blake say about her? But he's dead just the same. It may be all a coincidence, but when she wants men dead—they die! Strang, I can't fit her into the picture at all. Despite her associations, she seems a—well, a lady."

Strang's eyes blazed brightly again. He said:

"A lady, yes. The Lady of Death."

7

MAXIE GETS THE BREAKS

DESPITE THE UNDERSTANDING that Maxie was dying on his feet, those same feet made fast time once Maxie had descended in the automatic lift to the basement of the huge apartment house. He was out the basement exit, twisting through the court, and finally on the street to the right of the building.

Maxie didn't run once he was on that side street. In fact, he leaned against a street pole and drew in long slow breaths. He cursed slightly, too, as he felt the trembling in his legs just beneath the knees. Maxie had been an athlete. These sudden spells of weakness, the cold perspiration from little exertion or excitement were new to him. Besides, for the first time in his life Maxie felt fear. Not fear of death by the hands of these desperate killers that Strang hunted. Maxie was used to the idea of death long before he began to work for Mr. Strang.

When Strang had opened several small offices, which he often used in his campaign against parole violators and those who controlled the parole racket—hidden, secret places watched over by a single individual—Maxie had been one of the first to join forces with Strang. He had interviewed many of those others who came after him—men and women who came in response to a care-fully worded ad in the paper. And those men and women he had hired for Strang had been found by Quinn; killed by Quinn's people. Maxie was the only one left. Maxie, who lived with and worked directly for Strang, remained unharmed.

Maxie didn't fear that Johnny Lester would get away from him, so he didn't run; simply walked rapidly when he left the support of the pole. He had sufficient time. For he knew that Lester's car was parked several blocks from the apartment house, while his was just down the street. He had been close behind Lester when the gunman broke into Strang's apartment. Maxie had been watching for Lester—was prepared for him. Lester had circled that block several times before parking. So Maxie had simply driven on, left his own car on the side street, and was in the apartment a good five minutes before Lester came.

Strang was right, as usual. The trap was set, and although it had taken the best part of two weeks, Johnny Lester had finally walked straight into it.

As for the girl, Resa Kent, being in that apartment when he entered, Maxie had not known it then and did not know now. When he entered the apartment ahead of Lester, he had gone straight to the picture and stepped into the hidden recess behind it.

Maxie reached his car. He nodded his satisfaction. The big black sedan was still parked far down the block. Johnny Lester had not yet— But he had. The black car was moving. Maxie slid under the wheel, into gear and followed slowly, then increased his speed as the car ahead turned the corner.

A minute later, as he sped down Centre Street, he had no doubt that Johnny Lester was in a hurry.

AND JOHNNY LESTER in a hurry, was much easier to follow. Maxie had little trouble keeping the speeding car in sight. Taxis shot in and out, to be sure, but the breaks were even for the big car Maxie followed and the little one he drove.

Johnny Lester shot around another corner. Maxie was just in time to see him cross the street intersection a block down, and stepping on the gas he shot in pursuit. There were two more turns before Lester reached the other side of the city, and at the final turn Maxie just avoided trouble; avoided it by a sharp twist of the wheel, the squeal of protesting tires as his car shot straight ahead. For, just as he was about to swing that corner in pursuit of Lester's car, he saw the tail light; saw Lester's car stop at the curb.

Maxie passed him, swung around the next corner, doubled back beyond the other end of the block where Lester was parked, and finding a dark spot, jerked to a stop. Almost at once he was out of the car, hurrying to the corner. There was something familiar about the street, but he was not certain of it then.

Maxie turned the corner, pressed his body tightly against the dark brick of a building and peered the length of the block. The big car was there. Dully he made it out in the shadows as he moved along close to a row of brownstone fronts, each house very much like the other.

Moving furtively in the protecting shadows, he recognized the street; recognized a house several numbers down and on the opposite side of the street. Though it was an exact duplicate of the other houses it had, over the years, assumed a formidable appearance. The small, knee-high stone wall in front had given place to a high, spiked fence. The simple green shutters that had in years gone by protected rooms from the sun, now protected the windows from the entrance of undesirable and uninvited visitors. They were made of heavy steel and were swung tightly across the windows. It was the house of Sam Silverman.

Maxie worked his way down that side street until he was almost opposite Silverman's. Then he slid up the steps of a dark house, and slipping behind the grille work of the old porch waited, his attention divided between the house of Sam Silverman and the dark sedan almost half a block away.

Five, ten, fifteen minutes he waited, lying flat on the tiny porch. Then, Silverman's front door was slowly opening. But it was not Johnny Lester who came out; it was not old Sam Silverman.

The man paused almost in the center of that open door, turned up his coat collar, pulled down his hat and tucked a stick under his arm. He took one step forward, closed the door swiftly. After a quick look up and down the street he descended the steps and walked rapidly toward the car by the corner.

And Maxie came to life. There was no doubt now who Johnny Lester was waiting for, and if Maxie wished to see where they went he would have to be fast. He would have to reach his own car before Lester's black sedan turned that corner.

HE MADE IT all right and was surprised to find that his legs were steady and his heart, though raising the very devil inside his chest, held out. He was in the car, the motor purring, when the black sedan swung the corner and turned right. And this time the big car had a passenger—Martin Quinn.

Maxie felt better, much better. What if it was his last night? It might turn out a big one—an important one. Quinn and Silverman and Lester! The big three of the parole racket. He smacked his lips. Only one more to complete the four leaders. Just one more! Just Senator Robert Carson Stone.

Exactly twenty-two minutes later Maxie saw the car ahead pull to the curb a few doors below the Senator's house.

Maxie saw Martin Quinn leave the car and, walking fast, mount the front steps of Senator Stone's house. Then Johnny Lester drove away and Maxie followed him.

Maxie felt pretty good. Certainly he was getting the breaks. He didn't stop to figure just how many breaks he had gotten that night, and although he caught a flash of Martin Quinn standing on the steps of Senator Stone's house when he sped by in pursuit of Lester, he didn't figure why Quinn was still there despite the fact that a good minute, perhaps two, had passed since Maxie had returned to his own car, to take up the trail again.

Maxie had but one thought. His riding that night had definitely linked up the four big men in the parole racket. Strang had known of that association, of course. But here, in the course of half an hour, all four of them had made connections.

Yes, Maxie felt that he had done well and that he knew a lot of things. But one thing he didn't know was—that Quinn had left the steps of Senator Stone's house, returned to the car, spoken a few quick sentences to Johnny Lester and was back on the steps again when Maxie shot by. Yes, Maxie knew that he was on the steps, but not "again." Nor did he see Martin Quinn nod his head several times in apparent satisfaction as Maxie's tail light disappeared from view.

Maxie was having the breaks; all the breaks. But he was a little surprised and a little curious as he followed Lester. The big sedan turned out of the residential district, cut off the main arteries and started toward Conners Point, a little habited section of the city either day or night. Dark stores, deserted warehouses, and then a couple of lights. One a lunch room. The other, just across the road, a cigar store. But both were still open.

It was the lunch room that Lester sought, and Maxie a few minutes later was peering through the window watching Lester munching a hamburger, stirring coffee, leisurely lounging on a stool before the counter. He was to meet someone there, Maxie thought. And again his eyes drifted to the cigar store. The worn sign in front told of a telephone inside.

Maxie crossed the street. It would be a good time to make his report to Mr. Strang if, as he hoped, the cigar store contained a booth and not just an unenclosed pay phone.

ONCE INSIDE, MAXIE found the place to be a combination pool room and cigar store. Three or four men, playing pool in the back, were plainly visible through a partly drawn curtain. Maxie nodded as the proprietor, in shirt sleeves, came from between the curtains and went back behind them again as Maxie entered the telephone booth.

Maxie got his number. After a few seconds the voice of Mr. Strang came over the wire. Maxie hurriedly made his report. When he told of being across the street from Silverman's house, Strang interrupted.

"Silverman was murdered tonight, Maxie; probably while you were outside his house. You waited while Lester went in and did the job."

"Lester—Johnny Lester!" Maxie gasped. "Why, he never even entered Silverman's house. I can account for every minute of his time right up to when he left Quinn at Senator Stone's house, came back here to the lunch room across the street and—"

"Quinn! But where did he pick up Quinn, and—"

"I know, I know!" Maxie's voice was high pitched now—eager. "Quinn murdered Silverman! Johnny Lester didn't. Johnny—"

Maxie never knew why he stopped talking, or why he turned suddenly and looked through the glass door of that booth. But what he saw made his sunken eyes widen in deep sockets. He was looking straight at the evil face of Johnny Lester; at those cruel eyes just showing beneath the felt hat; at those sneering lips partly visible above the turned-up collar. Maxie thought of two things at once. The gun beneath his armpit and of Mr. Strang, who was anxiously calling his name over the phone.

But he knew his gun was useless. He read death there in Johnny Lester's eyes. He raised his voice slightly in the smallness of that booth. His words were simple and directed as if speaking to Johnny, who could only see his lips move, through the glass. But to Strang, at the other end of the wire, they were clear and loud. Those words were:

"It's Johnny Lester with a Tommy gun, boss. The wife and kid will now—"

Johnny Lester's jaws set, his eyes narrowed—and Maxie, the man who wanted to die by violence, dug his right hand beneath his left armpit. It wasn't in him to stand there and be shot to death, when the moment came. His hand went under his coat, grasped his gun, and drew it from its holster.

But even as he drew it Johnny Lester's finger had tensed on the trigger of his gun. Maxie's body jarred back and forth inside the booth, pounding against the rear partition as bullets drove into his chest, his shoulders and then his head. But Maxie's gun was found later gripped in his dead hand, when the several men—flat on the floor in that back room—finally came in.

8

COLD-BLOODED MURDER?

FOR ONCE THE iron nerves of Strang were shaken. He called into the phone. Words shouted back at him, but not his words. They were: "It's Johnny Lester with a Tommy gun. The wife and kid will now—"

Strang clicked the instrument several times, then dropped the phone back in its holder. He could not think clearly. He poured himself a stiff drink and downed it with one swallow. He smiled grimly. Maxie had wanted to die by violence. His wife and child were his first thought when he joined with Strang, his last one, too, when he—when he *left* Strang.

Strang reached for the phone again. Barton! His hand dropped to the table. No, there was nothing to tell Barton; nothing to tell him yet. Just a message over the phone, and death. A death that must receive immediate attention; personal attention. Johnny Lester had struck at Mr. Strang and at his mission when he killed Maxie, a man who served that mission.

He went to the decanter again, poured another drink, half raised the glass in salute.

Mechanically he felt the butt of the heavy police thirty-eight beneath his left armpit. He put on his hat and coat, walked with measured step down the hall. The back of his head was pounding slightly where that bullet was. Mr. Strang was in action again. He was going out into the night to kill. He knew that, and he laughed. His lips twisted and quivered like an animal's. Far back—so deep in his eyes that it was as if one looked at it through the wrong end of binoculars, the burning fires were there.

He reached the door, turned the knob. He was going into the night to kill. But no one could call it coldblooded murder. Exterminating a rat—a human rat—couldn't rightly be called murder.

Strang jerked the door open with his left hand, raised the gun in his right coat pocket, half closed a finger upon the trigger.

The girl never moved. Cold eyes rested on his hot ones, a white face remained hard. Red lips parted. Resa Kent said:

"So you're going to kill. Let me inside. I want to talk to you."

Strang never moved. His finger never left the trigger of the gun. But he had to clear his throat before he spoke.

"Then you know Maxie was shot to death." Strang hesitated. "Knew it before he was killed. It was less than ten minutes ago."

The girl's eyebrows lifted, her lips parted.

"Maxie! I liked him, too. He was very loyal. No, I didn't know he was dead—was killed."

Strang backed into the hall. The girl followed; the door closed. Strang said:

"Then why the statement? Not a question, but a statement—that I was going to kill."

HER SHOULDERS MOVED.

"You've seen the movie of *Doctor Jekyll and Mr. Hyde*, haven't you? When you saw Hyde's face you didn't have to know the circumstances. When I saw yours, I didn't, either. That calm cool deliberate mission of yours will blow up if you let things get you like that. Why—a child would have read it in your face, as in any gunman's face. There was murder in your eyes; in the hand you held in your pocket."

"No!" Strang said. "No, not murder." He backed toward the living room, the girl following him. Yet he knew that she spoke the truth. Again the thumping in his head; again the doubt in his eyes. The ever present fear of madness.

He allowed the girl to push by him, watched as she crossed the living room, saw her take the bag from beneath her arm and toss it onto the couch. Then she said:

"If you fear me, my gun's in the bag." And half-turning her back on him she began slowly removing her gloves. "You may be interested to know that I got to Reardon in time. Sergeant Joseph Cooper is not a man to be trusted with secrets."

Strang shrugged his shoulders. She was so cold and beautiful that it seemed to calm him. He said, simply and truthfully:

"I was very fond of Maxie. Johnny Lester killed him. You didn't know that?"

"No," she kept her eyes on his, "I didn't know that."

"You didn't know that death struck twice tonight? You didn't know that Silverman—Sam Silverman was murdered?"

Her eyes widened, red lips curved slightly.

"So Sam Silverman is dead! No, I didn't know that he is

dead, but I thought—" She paused, then nodded her head. "Yes, I thought he would be."

"You didn't plan it?"

"Plan it!" Shoulders shrugged. "No, I wouldn't say that."

Strang set steady eyes on the girl, spoke quick, jerky words.

"You gave Barton the information that would convict Silverman. You told Barton the best time for the raid. Barton made the raid; he found Silverman dead. You gave the information of the raid to Quinn and Quinn killed Silverman so that he wouldn't talk."

"That," she said, "would be very hard to prove."

"As all truth against political and protected criminals is hard to prove."

The girl was seated now; Strang stood above her. She laid a hand upon the fingers he placed on the arm of the chair. Her voice was soft and low.

"You remember the finding of Olga Keith's body? Oh! I know she was of the half world; she never had a chance to be anything else. But she helped me here in the city when I first came." Resa Kent's smile was rather cynical. "I hoped to save her at the end as you may have hoped to save others.

"Sam Silverman murdered her; placed his bony hands about her neck and choked her slowly to death. I won't go into the details nor the reasons; they are too revolting. I warned her not to go there that night. It was Lester who brought her there. She was very fond of Lester. He liked money *more*."

The girl's hands came far apart; there was a misty look in her eyes. "You mustn't judge me, Strang. You and I play too far outside the laws of man. You can't judge me. Yes, I put the thoughts into the minds of men that caused Silverman's death. I am not sorry."

Strang looked at the girl. For a moment he thought that he saw something different in that white face. At least, something back in her eyes; behind the steady coldness of them. But if he did, it was gone at once. She said:

"Tell me about tonight." And this time Strang was sure that the coldness of her fingers upon the back of his hand became warm. "Tell me about Maxie."

STRANG TOLD HER. If he trusted her or not he did not know. She sat there so stiff and straight before him. The Lady of Death! But what he knew, she could know—would know. There was nothing he could tell her that Johnny Lester couldn't report to Quinn.

Her face remained the same while he talked, but her body seemed to grow tense—tighten. When he told her of the last words of Maxie and the clear staccato notes of the machine gun fire over the wire, her upper teeth settled firmly on her lower lip. When he had finished, the hand that gripped his closed; claw-like crimson nails bit deep into his flesh. It was some time before she spoke. Then when the words finally came, she looked past him; over his shoulder.

"What a terrible thing—what an awful thing life can be. And you and I, like strangers from another world, are thrown into it. What huge hands Quinn can stretch out, and—" She stopped suddenly; then, "You can't do it alone, Strang. You can't get convictions until crime and politics are split. The Bar Association has tried and failed. Commissions on crime, eminent men who have spoken to the public from platform and pulpit—all have failed."

"I haven't failed." His eyes burned again now. "I can't fail."

"But you should have started right at the head of the evil system. Quinn or the man above him, if there is such a man. You've worked wrong. If you had cut off the head, the body could not act."

Strang looked steadily at her, shook his head.

"That is where you are wrong; where all who have fought against crime were wrong. There is a belief that if you get the leader of the racket, you get the racket itself. That is a fallacy; a fallacy that the big cities, as well as the small towns, that sometimes the national, as well as the state governments, have believed in. But there never was a leader without someone close enough to him to take his place; who wanted to take his place. When you eliminate a leader you simply pass the leadership down the line, but the great organization that that leadership has built up still remains.

"Don't you see, Resa? I first sent to prison, to the electric chair, and even to quick death at the hands of the police, many of those who believed in this leader or series of leaders. The little rats began to understand that the protection they enjoyed could not always be counted on. After undermining the confidence of the many, I worked up to those few in command who some day hoped to control. Finally, I have come to those closest to the leader. Steve Blake was one; he is dead. Sam—" He paused.

The girl nodded.

"Sam Silverman was another. He, too, is dead."

Strang nodded.

"Johnny Lester is the next. Don't you see my plan?"

"Lester and Quinn still remain," the girl said, half aloud.

"Lester and Quinn—and Senator Stone. When the final one is gone, nothing but confusion will be left behind. There will be no under-man familiar enough or trusted enough or capable enough to step in."

"I see," the girl said. "Then you want these men dead."

Strang nodded very slowly.

"Yes, I suppose that is it. I want these men dead or in prison."

"And you intend to kill them?"

"I do not intend to commit murder, if that's what you mean."

"But you intended to commit murder a few minutes ago, when I saw you at the door. Johnny Lester has used a gun all his life. He is quick; he is sure." She looked into his eyes. "No!" she finally said. "I can't let you do it. Johnny's too fast."

Strang laughed. The girl shivered slightly. That laugh always bothered her. She decided suddenly.

"Very well," she said. "I will deliver Johnny Lester to you. Will you trust me?"

STRANG'S EYES NARROWED, his lips parted. His narrow eyes met her brown ones. They were soft and warm, and the marble was seemingly gone from her face. But it was the look in her eyes—the same look he had seen there when Blake had died. Well, he had wanted Blake dead. But there was Barton and Quinn and the dead Silverman. All had trusted her one time or another. All might have looked into her brown eyes and— But she went on talking without waiting for an answer.

"I have a plan. You must leave here. Go to the Saint Mortimer Hotel, register as—oh—Edward Jordan.

Edward Jordan!" She repeated the name as if to make it register in her mind as well as his. "I'll telephone you there. But stay in your room; stay away from Barton. It won't be long. Perhaps tomorrow night. Don't question me. I don't know exactly how, but I'll deliver Lester to you one way or another. If you're the man you pretend to be you can make him talk, or—"

She turned from him, lifted the bag from the couch, pulled on her gloves, swung back as he came to his feet.

"You trust me, of course," she said.

He looked at her eyes, then avoided them. Involuntarily his glance fell to her handbag, stayed on the bag. But he spoke the truth; or at least, started to speak it as he raised his eyes.

"If it were just myself I would trust you, but—"

"I know. I know! It is your cause; your mission." There was a slight mockery in her voice. "You said that before, said it over and over. I'm offering you Lester—Johnny Lester, who killed Maxie. Well—I've worked with you before. I've hated as much as you've hated."

"And you said that before—that you hated where I hated, but you loved where I did not love. Something like that! I did not understand it."

"You know where you hate." She moved close to him. "So you know where I hate." Brown eyes found his and this time held them.

Suddenly she did it. Threw both arms about his neck. Soft lips pressed against his; lips that had nothing of marble to them. Then her arms dropped, her body swung, and she moved rapidly to the hall.

"Edward Jordan!" She flung the words back over her shoulder. "Hotel Saint Mortimer!"

Strang stood there and watched her go. He didn't understand his own feelings. For years his heart had held nothing but hate; it still held that hate. He thought there was room for nothing else. Yet, suddenly there was something else there—something new and warm and alive.

But Resa Kent! Could he trust her? Had she lied when she spoke of love; had she lied when her lips— But he didn't think she lied then. And he shook his head. He wasn't reasoning now, he told himself; at least, he wasn't reasoning as a man with such a mission should reason. He didn't quite understand it himself. Perhaps, inside of him, something that had been dead for a long time was living again. Perhaps, unknowingly, he wanted it to live.

STRANG PACED HIS room in the Saint Mortimer Hotel the next day. The killing of Maxie was given little newspaper attention. The promotion of Barton from inspector to chief inspector ran far over on the inside of the paper. There was Barton's record of sudden achievement in the past two years, entirely accounted for by the free hand given him by the new administration. Strang liked that. His smile was real.

And he had received the call from the girl. She had said on the phone that the trap was set; that he'd have a chance of making Lester talk. But she wouldn't tell him the time of the meeting or the place, yet. Why? Yes, he had asked that. And she had said simply that she didn't know. That he was to wait for a call from her between ten and eleven that night. He had started to tell her flatly that he wouldn't be there. But he hadn't told her. As he hesitated she had clicked up the receiver.

But he was there by the phone in his room all evening, He was thinking of Blake. He was thinking of that kiss. The kiss of death? And he was thinking, too; thinking almost as the phone rang, that Resa Kent might be at that very moment in the arms of Lester—Johnny Lester, who was waiting to be killed.

When he heard her voice over the phone he said just the opposite of what he had expected to say. He had said simply:

"Give me the layout, and I'll come."

"Good!" she answered. "Listen very carefully." And after she had given him full directions, "Now repeat them to me."

Strang repeated the words very slowly. He didn't like them. It was a lonely spot outside the city limits. A bungalow far from other dwellings.

"That's right." And then her voice changed—softened. "And, Strang, believe in me. Remember last night, just before I left. Park your car as I said, walk straight to the front door. You will find it unlocked. There will be a light inside. Walk straight across the living room and go up the stairs. Your life—my life depends on your coming, and doing exactly as I say."

"And Johnny Lester will be there—then?"

The girl hesitated, and Strang didn't like it.

"No!" she finally said. "We'll arrange for his reception later."

"Why will he come later?"

"Because," she said slowly, "I will be there waiting for him, too."

And that was all. He was "coming." Johnny Lester was "coming." He shook his head, trying to dismiss the thought that perhaps Johnny Lester believed in her eyes; maybe even in her lips, too. And one of them had to be wrong that night.

9

THE DEATH TRAP

RESA KENT FINALLY swung, and faced Johnny Lester.

"It wasn't in the bargain that I should stay here," she said. "I have a good mind to walk out on you, threat or no threat."

"Try it, if you'd like your face punched in." There was no rancor in his voice as Johnny looked up from an easy chair. "But I thought you hated him, wanted to see him die." And suddenly, "It's like this, sister. I never trust women. You've done a nice job, and the worst of it wasn't getting Quinn to put a bigger price on Strang's head. I want a witness to the shooting."

The girl shrugged. "All right. I stay. But don't forget my 'cut,' and don't forget to make him talk."

"So you want your 'cut.' It wasn't just your fancy for me, then?" He grinned.

"Hardly." The girl looked directly at Johnny Lester. "You don't go in strong for women."

"Oh! I can take them or leave them alone." Johnny moved his shoulders, came to his feet and walked over to the tool chest by the corner. The girl's eyes widened as he opened it and lifted out the heavy chunk of steel. She cried out:

"No, Johnny. Not a machine gun. You can't do that, Johnny."

"Why not?" He looked at her from under heavy lids. "It's quiet here." He patted the Thompson machine gun. "There's one thing sure about this baby. When you kill a man with it, he stays dead. He don't pop up in court later to put the finger on you."

The girl's brown eyes widened; the marble whiteness came into her face.

"You're not man enough to use an ordinary rod, even when his back will be to you."

"I don't know about being 'man enough,' but I'm not fool enough. Where did you ever get the idea that I go in for this hero stuff, Beautiful? This Strang is fast with a gun. Sure, I know that!"

The girl sneered; there was nothing of breeding in her face now.

"Strang comes in, crosses to the stairs—and you don't think an ordinary gun is enough. You've got to use a machine gun!"

"That's right!" Lester grinned evilly. "If you ever go for me in a big way, remember I'm not sensational—just reliable. This guy, Blake—I'm not sorry he took the dose, but he could shoot rings around me with an ordinary rod. Yet Strang puts those burning eyes of his on him, does a quick flop across a table, picks up a gun and lets Blake have it. So what? Strang gets a couple of slugs dug out of him, and they throw dirt in Blake's face."

"Then you won't make him talk—tell where he gets all his information about Quinn!"

"I'll give him his chance to squeal. But he won't do any of that movie gunplay-business with me."

"If you use a machine gun, we'll have to leave him here afterward."

"Certainly!" Lester agreed. "You've been reading the papers, kid. 'Killed here and thrown out of the car there.' I never did it; never will do it. 'He lies where he dies' is my motto. He might lie here for days."

He walked over to the girl, looked at her steadily. "I oughta slam you in the mouth and tie you up until after it's over. You women are all the same. Never know your minds—always changing your minds at the last minute. Well, this 'kill' is going according to schedule. I never had any luck making changes."

The girl was watching him, but her face was expressionless.

"You'll shoot him in the back on the stairs?" she asked.

"No. You say he'll follow your directions, and I was with you when you gave them. I squat there in the kitchen," he shot out a finger. "Mr. Strang opens the door, walks across the room and reaches the stairs. He'll be off balance halfway up then. That's when I'll step into the picture; just halt him with his back to me; make him drop his hardware and turn around. Does he carry one or two guns?"

"He'll probably carry two guns tonight. I'm sure he had one in his coat pocket when I saw him at the door last night. Where will I be?"

Lester considered.

"In the dining room. It's dark. We'll leave by that window." And as she moved across the room and lifted her pocketbook he added, "I lifted your gun out of there."

"Why?"

Lester shrugged his shoulders.

"Women shouldn't have heaters. They do things they don't mean to do, just like they talk. I had a dame once—" He looked at her. "Hell, don't get all hot over it. You can have it back afterward. I had a girl run out with one of them toy pistols once because she hated the guy I was going to 'get.' What happened? She shot him twice in the chest, got between my Tommy and him and gave him a chance to draw."

"Well—you're still alive."

Lester laughed.

"Yeah. But she ain't. Nice kid, too. But I had to blast her out with him; there was no other way."

"You don't think it would be better to get him right as he comes in the door?" the girl asked suddenly.

"Damn it to hell!" Lester raised his voice. "It was you who suggested the stairs, and the 'talk.' I can't mow him down first and then make him talk. What the hell's come over you?"

"Do you think he'll talk?"

"I don't know. Some guys do when they face a Tommy."

"But you'll kill him, talk or no talk?"

"If he's willing to talk I'll listen, then—" And Lester laughed. "This guy must have something 'big' on you— or he has another skirt, you want him dead so bad. Don't worry! After he spills his guts, I'll spill them right. Come on! Get in that dining room—not too near the kitchen door."

Lester watched her go, looked up the stairs and saw that the trap above, to the unfinished attic, was closed.

After that—silence, except for Johnny's occasional whisper:

"Still there, kid? All right!" And her answer:

"Still here—all right. Be sure he talks."

Lester's laugh was low.

"Quinn picked a wise one in you. If I don't make him talk you'll wise Quinn up, eh?"

"I'll wise Quinn up if you don't make him talk. Mr. Strang knows something I want to know."

Lester's laugh was just as low, but not so pleasant. He said:

"I knew I should have slapped you away. Sh—s!"

Lester's voice died. Just a dull "sh—s" and silence. Feet beat across wood outside, stopped. A knob rattled, turned with a dull click. The door was opening.

10

ON THE ATTIC STAIRS

IF STRANG WONDERED at times if he was a little mad, he perhaps wondered more so now as he parked his car in the dark side lane. He could see the light in the bungalow. It was far back among the trees. Certainly a nice place for a talk; a nice place to make a man talk, and a nice place, too, for stopping a man from talking—forever.

And what brought him on that dangerous journey? The brown of the girl's eyes; the warmth of her lips, the honesty of her hate and her love? He had come because he had to know the truth about the girl. He had to know if she lied to him. And he wanted Johnny Lester's life.

He was on the porch, his hand upon the door knob. He was going to obey her instructions to the letter. Enter, cross the living room and mount the stairs!

He closed the door behind him, hesitated only a second, then stepped into the lighted room, his right hand deep in his coat pocket gripping a gun, his index finger wound about the trigger of that gun. His eyes never missed a thing in it. The chairs, the couch, the table, the vase with the artificial flowers upon the mantel, the dark entrance to the dining room. Quickly he crossed to the stairs by the darkness of the kitchen and started up them. He had almost reached the top when it happened.

Strang froze there upon the steps. The girl had double-crossed him. He had double-crossed his mission. The voice said:

"The same machine that wiped out friend Maxie is almost smack against your back. If you want to find out how it works, make a wrong move."

Strang didn't move. He said, and the words were just forced from his lips:

"Johnny Lester! So she trapped me!"

"Correct, both times!" Lester said behind him. "The great Mr. Strang, the feared Mr. Strang, the killer—is, after all, just a sucker for a woman. Now—lift your right hand from your pocket. Let the gun fall. That's right, just drop it on the stairs." And as the gun thudded on wood, "Now turn, both your hands at your sides."

Strang turned and faced Johnny Lester. Lester looked full into those eyes; the burning hatred of them.

And despite the machine gun in his hands, Lester felt a shiver of fear. He said: "Now raise those hands above your head. You're not going to get a chance to pull out another rod."

STRANG DIDN'T SPEAK. He saw the nose of that Tommy gun, the steady, expert hands that held it, the evil of the face behind it and he raised his hands slowly above his head.

Lester watched Strang without speaking. He rather liked the situation. It appealed to him. He waited for Strang to break; for his knees to give; for his whine. They would be old, familiar signs to Lester. He had seen many men—hard, swaggering, desperate killers, fall to their knees on a lonely road; beg and plead and sometimes start to run screaming away. He got a kick out of it, too. But this man simply looked at him. Lester wanted the man to break before he gave it to him.

Without turning his head, Lester raised his voice suddenly and called out:

"Want to take a look at him, sweetheart?" He listened. There was no answer. Only silence from the dining room.

There was a sudden draft of air. It was cool, fresh. It came through the swing door that led to the dining room; a door he had put chairs against so the girl couldn't jam things up by passing through that way. Lester's face reddened and he cursed as he realized the significance of that sudden draft.

Strang stood there looking down on the man. The girl had brought him to his death but did not care to stay and see him die. He stood there, his hands above his head, his fingers touching the ceiling above the stairs. It was then he discovered the trap door to the attic. He felt it with his fingers. His hands and fingers were well out of sight of Lester's steady glare.

Hope there! A possible chance to escape. Slowly he stretched his arms upward—pressed his fingers against the trap door. It gave slightly; then held tightly.

Lester was saying:

"The damn girl fainted, or took a run-out powder on me. Well, Mister, I don't suppose you want to talk and tell me where you get all your information?" And with a chuckle, "I've got to warn you that anything you say will be used against you."

"I have nothing to say." And Strang paused. The trap door above had suddenly given under the pressure of his fingers! No, it hadn't "given." It was lifting itself; he wasn't even touching it. And then something brushed his fingers. It was hard and cold. His fingers gripped it, closed around the barrel of a gun.

Lester said, in a resigned voice:

"Since there ain't any audience—and you don't want to talk—I might as well get it over. Right in the stomach, Mr.—"

"Stop!" Strang cried out. "I'll talk—I'll talk."

Lester's head nodded, his eyes narrowed. This was what he wanted. He liked to hear them squeal before they died. His lips twisted. He pushed the nose of the Tommy gun closer.

"Right in the belly," Lester said again, and again Strang cried out.

STRANG DIDN'T KNOW what he was saying; he didn't care. He was stalling for time. Tensely his fingers gripped the heavy steel of a thirty-eight revolver. Held it there above his head. In the darkness, where Johnny Lester could not see it.

And he said in a calm, even voice as he looked away from Lester out into the dining room:

"So you came to see me die after all, Resa Kent."

Only a fraction of a second did Johnny Lester move his eyes; only a darting, half involuntary glance. But that split second was enough. Strang Cummings had swiftly considered a number of things. Perhaps Resa Kent was playing the same trick on him that she had played on Blake. Was the gun in his hand loaded? If it wasn't or if it was filled with blanks, then—

Strang laughed. There was but one thing to do. He jerked down that right hand and the gun that it held.

There was a roar; just a single shot—then silence.

Strang saw the hole almost directly in the center of Lester's forehead; and he knew that, though the eyes of Lester still glared, that those eyes didn't see him; didn't see anything. They never would see anything again.

Johnny Lester still stood upon his feet. Strang stretched out a hand, gripped the long nose of the machine gun. Then, like a contortionist, Johnny Lester sank slowly to the floor and lay still.

"The Lady of Death," Strang muttered, half aloud. And, turning, looked up into the darkness of the attic.

"You played it pretty close that time," he started, stopped, ducked his head. The trap door above fell with a crash.

A voice spoke, seemingly only a whisper. Strang quit his effort to listen. The voice said:

"You don't know just how close it was played, Strang. I had the gun hidden in the attic, but there was a time I didn't think I was going to get to it."

He waited for more but it didn't come. Then he drove his shoulder hard against the trap door. It gave, raised little by little; but he had trouble moving the trunk which had been pulled upon it. When he did climb into the attic he had more trouble, stumbling over things in the darkness. Finally he reached an open window. There was a ladder below it. Something outside caught his eye. It was a figure running in the moonlight; a figure that quickly disappeared behind a grove of trees. In a moment there came the soft purr of a motor.

BEHIND THE CURTAIN

*Ten Minutes for the Job and Someone
Else Would Handle the Body—Martin
Quinn Had It All Figured Out. But
He Hadn't Figured on Mr. Strang*

1

DEATH STRIKES SUDDENLY

MR. STRANG SAT straight and stiff in the dining booth at the rear of the long restaurant. He even tried to push himself farther back in the slight dimness of the corner as his burning eyes settled on the face of Chief Inspector James Barton. But Barton swung suddenly, leaned forward and stared at that hard, gaunt face.

"Fancy meeting you here," Barton said lightly, and as Strang eased over closer to the wall, Barton slid in beside him.

Strang never took his eyes off the Inspector's. There was no humor in his voice when he spoke.

"You are not trying to give me the impression that your finding me here was a coincidence, *Chief Inspector* James Barton."

Barton reddened slightly, cleared his throat, finally said:

"I am not going to discuss finding you here at all. And I am Chief Inspector. I was pushed to that position by you; by your information that led directly to the arrests and sometimes to the deaths of our most vicious criminals—criminals on parole. And I don't mean death by police bullets only—I mean death directly by your hand.

You have not only killed men, but you have put me in a position where I owe you everything."

Mr. Strang shrugged his shoulders, leaned forward. His eyes were burning brightly now, his cheeks drawn.

"Don't worry about gratitude. I made use of you for my own ends. Through you and my own methods of striking I have burnt my words of vengeance into the headlines of the newspapers—into the editorials of those papers—into the minds of the people. 'Correct the Parole Evil!' has become a familiar slogan."

James Barton nodded.

"You are 'Mr. Strang' to the underworld," he spoke slowly. "To that part of the underworld controlled by Martin Quinn—Martin Quinn who has made a racket of the Parole System of our state. Martin Quinn who frees our most vicious criminals so that they may sin again. It

He leaned forward over the desk and grasped frantically for the gun

must be two years since you first telephoned me; gave me your name, Mr. Strang, and also gave me the name of a wanted murderer, the proof of his crime, his hideout and his record as a parole violator. Many calls after that—and finally our meeting. Mr. Strang, who struck terror into Martin Quinn and his organization. But now you are known to Quinn and to me as Strang Cummings, owner of the Modern Art Gallery. You are right out in the open. You are inviting death."

"Well," said Mr. Strang, "it is my death. Martin Quinn will have to kill me quickly if he wants to save his own skin, for I am getting ready to strike at the leaders of the organization."

"The leaders? You mean the leader—Martin Quinn."

"I mean Quinn, yes," Mr. Strang said slowly. "And I

mean also the man who controls Quinn, Senator Robert
Carson Stone."

"I tell you," Barton very nearly banged his fist upon the
table, "Senator Stone is an honest, a fine man. Besides, I've
had him watched day and night."

Mr. Strang laughed. At least Barton took it for a
laugh—a grating noise somewhere back in Strang's throat.
Strang said,

"You had Quinn watched, too, and the dead fence,
Silverman; also Johnny Lester and Blake. They are all dead,
but Quinn—yet what did you discover?"

Barton's hands came far apart.

"You're a hard man to reason with, Strang. Senator
Stone is seen with Quinn, of course, but he thinks Quinn
a straight shooter. Big men pat Quinn on the back. He
brings out the vote. That's just politics."

Strang said sharply, "I never gave you a bad steer. I'm not
giving you one now. Quinn must die, and Stone must be
convicted. We've wiped out the links between them and
the great parole racket they control."

BARTON DID NOT argue that point further. He thought
of the bullet there in Mr. Strang's head, close to his brain.
That bullet which might kill him if it remained there much
longer. And he shuddered too as he thought of the reason
for its remaining there. Of Strang's reason—Strang's fear
that the removal of that bullet might take away his lust to
kill, his mania for vengeance, his fetish against the present
parole evil, and his fear that madness or death might beat
him to the final curtain.

Inspector Barton looked at those burning eyes.

"All right." He shrugged heavy, tired shoulders. "You

made me. I owe you my job, and I'll go down with you if that's how it is to be. But I can't go down with you if you don't live."

Strang's lips curved. His left hand tapped beneath his right armpit. His right hand remained tightly fastened upon the bunched napkin as if he held taut.

Barton continued:

"Why not take another name? Perhaps your real name?"

"So—" said Mr. Strang, "my real name is not Mr. Strang—and now you surmise it is not Mr. Strang Cummings."

"I never surmise," said Barton. "Mr. Strang was a voice on the phone—a shadow of fear in the underworld that killed in the night. Mr. Strang Cummings is a public-spirited citizen who dealt in art in Paris and whose genius lay in buying the paintings of the unknown of today to have others discover and pay handsomely for them as celebrities of tomorrow. No, there must be a third person, for Strang Cummings was never heard of in Paris until a few years ago."

"So—" Mr. Strang's words seemed to come without his lips moving. "I pushed you up; forced an ambition into your honest carcass that never would have been there. And you repay me by digging into my past. Why?"

Barton's hands parted slightly.

"You were my friend," he said simply. "I wanted to know at the end where to ship your body." And when, even the hardened face of Mr. Strang seemed to relax—"Oh, come, Strang, there was no coincidence in my being here today. I came because you were to meet The Lady of Death."

"Resa Kent." Strang stiffened again. He was thinking of

the girl he had not trusted, whom both he and Barton had called the Lady of Death, for she had at that time caused the death of at least three men. The third not even Barton knew about, but he did suspect, for Barton said:

"Oh, I never asked you how Johnny Lester came to die with the machine gun in his hand. I have never even suggested that you killed him, though I know you must have. No one will miss him. But I would like to know if the Lady of Death—Resa Kent—was in at that killing."

Strang thought a long time before he answered. Resa Kent had arranged that killing—Resa Kent, who had very nearly cost Strang his life. But she had said she hated where Strang hated and that she loved him.

"Well—" said the Inspector, "remember the other deaths. You never knew if she wanted to save your life or to force you to take the life of another man. You—"

"There can be no mistake of her attitude toward me now." Strang remembered her eyes, her arms, that single moment her lips. The kiss that had stirred something within him, something he had never felt before—some soft spot he had been unaware of.

Inspector Barton turned his head to look directly at Strang.

"You are to meet her here today?"

STRANG BENT HIS wrist of the hand that still held the napkin. He gazed at the watch upon it; looked out of the booth at the empty tables of the departed luncheon guests. It was time for his meeting with Resa Kent.

"Yes," he said slowly. "Resa Kent is to be here, and she may be chancing her life to come. Since your back is to the main entrance she will not know of your presence here with me."

"I should think," said Barton, "that she might find it of considerable danger meeting you in a public place. She still works for—or at least associates with Martin Quinn."

"That's right," Strang agreed. "But I received a message from her asking me to be here. I had no way of warning her not to come—or suggesting another place. She might be in considerable danger."

Both men looked up. A man slid like a shadow into the booth—his hands stretched before him as he sat down opposite them. His face was white with prison pallor. His hands were white too, but for the twin, black, snubbed-nosed automatics they held; held far out—one covering Barton, one covering Strang—held so that they would not be seen by others outside the booth.

Barton said, "It's Killer Jackson! You went up for fourteen years for murder less than two years ago. I haven't seen you since."

Jackson sneered his answer:

"You'll see me for a few seconds anyway, that is if you keep both hands as they are—on the table. And the time was exactly two years ago today. The papers didn't publish my release, which explains why you didn't get it, flat-foot." Jackson's guns were very steady—his deep eyes very sharp, burning slightly but with a sudden fire. He liked to talk too. His tongue ran across his lips as if he enjoyed the sound of his own words.

"Well—" Barton spoke very quietly. "What's on your mind? You can talk to me without those rods. I never hounded a man who wanted to go straight." Calmly Barton sparred for time. Death seemed very close.

"I'll talk to you with a couple of doses of lead since you wanted to sit in on this rub-out. But it's the punk there I'm after."

Jackson glanced toward Strang, but his eyes watched both their hands.

Barton shook his head. His color had not even changed. The same healthy red was in his cheeks.

"You're too old a hand to kill a cop, Jackson." There was no tremor in Barton's voice. "You know that cop killers always burn, and you know what happens to them down-stairs in Headquarters before they burn—if they live to burn."

Strang slipped a side glance at Barton. He had always known that Barton did not fear death. But he knew also exactly what Barton was thinking—there were his two daughters. And Barton must have known that death was certain. But the man with the two guns was talking.

"Pretty smart, eh?" Jackson leaned a little forward now, his cheek bones protruding through his white skin. "I was let out of the stir for this particular job—to knock over Mr. Strang. No one knows me here. No one will suspect me. I'm working for a guy who knows how to set the stage. The swing door at the rear—a lad who's been planted in the kitchen, the street behind and—"

AND INSPECTOR JAMES Barton saw it all. Saw that death was certain and the killer's getaway sure. So if he had to die, he'd let others know who killed him. He could let out one yell to attract attention, but there were people in the front of that dining room. And Killer Jackson would place his back against that wall and shoot them down. He was a killer and desperate.

Barton's mouth clenched tight. Killer Jackson's eyes had narrowed to thin slits.

But it wasn't his eyes that Barton saw. It was the snub noses of those guns and the hands that held them. The knuckles of those trigger fingers were whitening—knuckles that were tightening as fingers closed.

The shot came. One shot? It sounded like one to Barton, but it must have been two. Just two fingers closing tightly together—two guns that exploded as one. Barton's eyes blinked. He stiffened for the pain, but there was no pain. Peculiar that—or was it? He had been shot before—twice before, and—

His eyes that had blinked snapped wide open. He was looking straight into the eyes of Jackson—eyes that still stared, but the stare was glassy. Jackson's hands had dropped to the table. There was the thud of the two guns, and Barton knew the truth. He was looking into the eyes of a dead man. A tiny purple hole had appeared almost directly in the center of the killer's forehead—a hole that was widening and turning red. It was then that Jackson pitched forward on the table.

People were shouting in the front of the dining room now. Feet were hurrying toward the door. Waiters were running about. And Mr. Strang came slowly to his feet. The hand that he stretched out to Barton did not tremble. The napkin that he held in it was burned and scarred and the black nose of a small gun peeked out of that hole. He spoke slowly as he tossed the napkin and the gun onto Barton's knees and wedged by him.

"It was your life as well as mine, Barton," he whispered hoarsely. "There will be credit in the death of Killer Jackson for you, only embarrassment for me. I had to shoot him through the head, of course."

"Of course—of course," Inspector Barton muttered as he came to his feet. And very low, as the manager came shouting down the room with two blue-coated figures, "You didn't exactly trust the Lady of Death then—eh, Strang?"

Strang half lowered his head as if he bowed.

"I would trust Resa Kent with my life," he said simply. "But I trust no man or woman with the life of my unfulfilled mission. Good day, Inspector."

Chief Inspector Barton shouted orders to the policeman as Mr. Strang walked slowly toward the street door.

"All right, boys—he's not in the show. The dead man is Killer Jackson—he was out to get me."

"Hell," said one of the cops. "Thought he was safe in stir"—and, seeing the head twisted grotesquely and the two guns still clutched in dead hands, "Some shooting, Inspector."

Barton looked at the dead man and nodded slowly. The two harnessed officers thought it was the first time the Inspector had ever paid himself a compliment. For Barton said very slowly,

"Some shooting is right."

2

SERGEANT COOPER
DOES HIS STUFF

MARTIN QUINN STOOD gazing out over the city. In the other room beyond the closed door of his private office girls worked steadily filing away imaginary certificates, writing letters and announcing the offer of high-priced bonds now handled by Martin Quinn, Inc.

In plain words, and in the language of Quinn's closest friends—it was by far the best front in the city. Martin Quinn, contrary to the accepted rules of criminals, picked no special type of crime, unless it was the Parole Racket, which he now favored both for the money that was in it and for the experts in a particular line of work which it afforded him.

He could supply a forger, a boxman, a diamond thief, an international spy, and he could produce killers of all grades right up to a homicidal maniac if the price was right. Yes— he could supply all these, for he knew where they were— kept safe and secure until Martin Quinn needed them. For they were behind the bars at the state prison. But Martin Quinn could arrange for certain "friends" to be turned loose by putting cash smack on the line in the right place.

Martin Quinn could supply himself with one other

thing. That was information—information from the mean-est source. A man who betrayed the people he served—the very law he had sworn to preserve. Sergeant Joseph Cooper, who, through the influence of Martin Quinn, was lifted from the pavements and given a soft berth at headquarters.

There was no doubt that Sergeant Joseph Cooper had welcomed the Quinn money. Cooper resented repeal and the income it lost him—a dollar a barrel for beer and a fair shakedown on the hard stuff if the prohibition officers didn't clean up the money before him.

Sergeant Cooper now stood patiently waiting as Martin Quinn spoke to him over his shoulder.

"You're not earning your feed despite the wads of bills I chuck your way. Come on—out with it. You're not suspected?"

"Slightly," Sergeant Cooper admitted.

"As I thought." The wrinkles on Quinn's neck worked in and out. "Listening at doors, I suppose. Probably caught bending in a hallway like any—"

"No—" Joseph Cooper interrupted sulkily. "It was the raid on Mr. Strang's apartment when he had Johnny Lester cornered. You told me, boss, and Johnny Lester gave me orders to follow him in if he was too long. I broke in the place—said it was police orders, and saved Johnny's life. Chief Inspector Barton's been asking me funny questions about it, that's all. I just been keeping quiet until things blow over. Nothing serious."

Quinn rubbed at his chin and let his little pop-eyes settle on Sergeant Cooper, at the same time remarking: "That's not like Barton. What the hell are you looking at?"

Sergeant Cooper didn't answer. He crossed to the huge

flat desk, looked down at the picture in the golden frame. He stared at it silently for a long time, finally asked:

"Where did you get that?"

Quinn walked across the room, patted Cooper on the back, almost boomed when he spoke.

"A queen, eh, Cooper? And that's the sort of girls you'll play around with if you do some real work for me." Quinn took the picture, held it off, looked at it. "Not like that maybe—not just like that. They don't come that way often." He looked quizzically at Cooper. "Knockout, eh?"

"Yeah." Cooper turned back from the window. He was not a young man, and the years had taught him to be careful. Finally he did speak. "You're not soft on that frail, are you?"

QUINN'S GREAT BULK stiffened, the clothes that had hung loosely on him suddenly seemed to fit his great frame. He was about to let off steam in no uncertain manner. But he didn't. Cooper spoke first.

"That dame," he said, "was in Mr. Strang's bedroom the night I made the raid. Oh—I'm not wrong. She has a swell pan that a lad would know any place."

Quinn placed the picture down on the desk again. He hesitated, finally said,

"Resa Kent, eh? In Strang's apartment? Strang, whose guts she hates." He stepped forward, moving rapidly. Huge hands went out and fastened on Cooper's shoulders. Quinn had strength—Cooper felt those fingers bite through his coat—into his flesh. "Why didn't you tell me before?"

"How could I? I never heard her name before." Cooper began to writhe slightly. He didn't like it. He was a man who struck out viciously when anyone laid a hand on him. Now he looked up at Quinn—even closed his fist. It wasn't Quinn's physical strength he was afraid of. It was his power. The power of money—politics. But he said, through clenched teeth, "There were two others with me—straight cops. Ask them."

Quinn's fingers dropped from the police sergeant's shoulder. He looked furtively around the room, spotted the bookcase, the screen beside it, and said to Cooper:

"She's outside now. Get behind that screen. I'll have her in and take a look at her. Don't come out unless I call you. She's a clever girl."

"But she'll deny it, boss. You'll have to get the others. If she's your—"

"She's not," Quinn said quickly, and added slowly, "Not yet." As Sergeant Cooper walked to the screen and stepped behind it, Martin Quinn pressed the buzzer on his desk. "Remember, not a peep unless I call you—" He stopped, addressed the tired-faced woman who opened the door. "Send Miss Kent in," he said abruptly.

Resa Kent took in the room with one quick glance of those sharp brown eyes. They were beautiful eyes, Quinn thought, but with a reservation. For occasionally she did tricks with them.

A strange coldness crept in. A cruel sort of hardness. He couldn't understand it. This girl had class. She represented to Quinn the other side of life that he mingled with, but never quite seemed to belong. Now she walked straight to the desk—picked up the picture of herself, said:

"Some guy with a twist for photography you dragged out of stir?" Her voice then was the hard voice of the night— the voice he didn't like. "You know I don't want my face standing up on a desk in your office or any other. How do you get that way?" She lifted the frame, smashed it to the floor, drew out her picture and tore it into tiny shreds.

There was no wrath in Quinn's little round eyes as he watched her. This woman was the only one who would stand up and slam it back at him word for word. It amused him. He rather liked it. And while he continued to like it, it would continue to amuse him.

THE GIRL LEANED back against the desk and faced Quinn. He spoke before she could.

"Don't be sore, Gorgeous." His lips parted in a smile. "You're a knockout when you're mad. There isn't a woman on the Avenue who wouldn't give her soul to have her map decorating that desk. I got a Rolls waiting for you, Beautiful, when you're ready to say the word."

The girl faced him squarely.

"I want to talk to you about Senator Stone now and—"

Quinn stopped her, first with a half movement of his hand, then with sudden quick words that put her on her guard. He said,

"I want to ask you about Mr. Strang. The terrible Mr. Strang," he sneered. "Seen him lately?"

"What has come over you?" she demanded. "I set him up for the—"

He stopped her again. He didn't want to discuss things with Cooper behind that screen. Certain ends of his organization knew only certain things. He wasn't in the habit of giving others the opportunity to have something on him. This time he said abruptly:

"Have you been to Strang's apartment?" He moved

closer to her, stretched out a hand, fastened it on her shoulder. His voice was loud now.

The girl shook herself free. Her brown eyes shot sparks. She straightened and stood stiff. But her eyes never faltered nor did her hands shake. She gave one quick glance toward the screen. She said:

"Yes, I was there." She stopped. "Sure, it was the night the cops raided the place. A lad called Cooper—a dumb cop—barged in."

"It was the night Johnny Lester was there, eh?" Quinn's lips curled slightly, viciously.

"Lester? I don't know. Strang Cummings built himself a bullet-proof room; it has a spring lock on it—can't be opened from the inside. Take a laugh if you want. I locked myself in. Strang hadn't come in yet. I was simply waiting for him."

"But you hate him—want to see him dead. By God, you told me he wouldn't touch you with a ten-foot pole since the Steve Blake kill."

"You told me to get in again with him. He wouldn't speak to me on the 'phone. He wouldn't receive me at his apartment. I crushed his place—" She shrugged her shoulders. "I'm not bad to look at. I just made a play."

"Did it work?" Quinn demanded.

"No—" the girl's face grew hard. "The cops weren't looking for me, because they simply walked out. But they followed me in pretty close. They put the clampers on the star act I hoped to play. You wouldn't want a dame hanging on your neck who filled the place with cops, would you?" She came close to him then, put her hands on his shoulders. "Listen, Quinn, it was Sergeant Cooper. He's a crooked cop. Inspector Barton must have had him trailing me and Strang must have slipped him a few hundred bucks to say I wasn't there. That's right. Cooper pretended to be looking for someone else, saw me, turned and beat it."

Quinn reached up and clutched her small, smooth hands, started to lift them from his shoulders, did slightly, but held them.

"Why didn't you tell me?" he asked.

HER EYES SHONE brightly. Her lips parted—they were very close to his—the closest they had ever been. Quinn thought of Cooper behind that screen and cursed inwardly. And the girl spoke.

"You didn't know I was making the play—and—" her shoulders shrugged, but her breath was warm and fresh against his face. "And I never report a failure."

Martin Quinn lifted her hands from close to his shoulders and placed them by her side. There was a certain hurt look in her eyes—something he had never seen there before. Damn it, the kid hadn't tried to duck out of the question. She had given him a straight answer. Damn Cooper, he thought. He led her to the door.

"Wait out there a couple of minutes, Kid," he said. "I want to talk to you, but I got to make a call first."

The girl held his arm tightly. "Sure, Quinn—and about this guy, Cooper. He's been giving information to Mr. Strang. Oh, I know—it has nothing to do with you—probably police business. Just thought I'd let you know. Johnny Lester tipped me to him. I was wondering if Cooper could have known Johnny's hideout before he died. I want to report on that Senator Stone—"

Martin Quinn shook his head. It was Cooper who

had told him that, despite the stories going around that a former gangster did Lester in, that it was actually Mr. Strang who killed Lester.

It was possible, of course, that Cooper might have heard this at police headquarters. But it was also possible that Cooper had tipped Mr. Strang on how to get Lester. Someone had tipped off a lot of things lately. And Cooper had tried to pin things on the girl.

Quinn was rubbing his chin as he closed the door and went back into his private office. Martin Quinn had a system that was hard and cruel, but efficient. He didn't need evidence as the law did to find a man guilty. He didn't even need proof. He just needed suspicion.

Cooper was a valuable man to Quinn. But he could also be a very dangerous one. Mr. Strang was plentifully supplied with money. Martin Quinn had no delusions about loyalty. He knew that Cooper had but one master. That master was greed. Well, maybe he'd have to pay Cooper more money—and again maybe he wouldn't. If Chief Inspector Barton had an eye on Cooper he wouldn't be worth much to Quinn.

Quinn looked coldly at Cooper as he walked into the room. Cooper said:

"She might have seen her picture and guessed I saw it and—and—" Cooper stopped. He knew that his reasoning was bad and he didn't have the slightest idea that it was actually the truth. "But I'm suspicious of that dame, boss. I think she's close to Mr. Strang, and I know a way to trap her into exposing herself."

Martin Quinn listened patiently to Cooper's strategy, and he nodded and patted Cooper on the back as he led him to the private door that gave directly onto the outer hall.

"I don't see how, with a mind like yours, you ever got on the police force at all." Quinn held an arm about the sergeant's shoulder. "It's clever. It's good." He thought a moment and nodded. "It's damn good. Now, we can't be seen together. Go down to the third block below the building. My car will pull to the curb. You get into it. I want to send you uptown." And when Cooper looked puzzled, "I've got a job for you—the easiest you ever had—and I'm so sure of you that the cash is in advance." He shoved a roll of bills into Cooper's hand. "Andy will be driving it."

He closed the private door and locked it, stretched slightly, sighed, then he lifted his gold-headed cane and twirled it in his fingers. When he was thinking he liked to be using his hands. Cooper's plan was clever, but it was far too elaborate and far too unnecessary with Resa Kent. Resa Kent—Martin Quinn smiled. It was a long time since he had gone for a dame like that. A little wild-cat, too. Well, he'd tame her. He was just about to press the button to have Miss Kent sent in—when he hesitated. Business before pleasure. He smiled grimly, lifted his private phone from a desk drawer and dialed a number.

"Martin speaking, Charlie," he said. "I'm sending a package up to you. Cooper." And, after a pause, "That's right, Sergeant Joseph Cooper." This time he paused for a full minute before he spoke. When he did speak his voice was soft and low. He said simply:

"I won't ever want to see him again, Charlie, and there's a roll on him that's all yours."

3

THE BUSINESS OF MURDER

THIS TIME WHEN Resa Kent came into the room she was all business. There were no hands upon Martin Quinn's shoulder; no soft breath against his face. He tried to put an arm about her, but she shook it off.

She said: "Well, I've gone through the Senator's papers and he's a careful man."

Quinn stopped his attempt to put an arm about the girl. He pulled at his several chins, rubbed his hands together, lifted a paper-weight from the desk and toyed with it.

"Listen, Kid," he talked hard facts now. "You've got looks. You've got brains. I fixed it up so you'd get the job with Senator Carson Stone. I didn't expect you'd get to his private papers, right off the bat."

The girl put her hands on her hips. "I chucked myself at him and when that didn't work and he seemed so busy I suggested I go to dinner with him—take dictation while he ate."

"And did you—you got him out to dinner, eh?"

"That's right." Resa Kent's brown eyes were cold now. "And what's more, I made the notes—made them while he ate. He's got a forest preservation bill, fires, insects— You're up the wrong tree, Martin. I think he's on to you.

Listen, everybody knows he's the big hand that moves you. He's no Silverman."

Martin Quinn stiffened. Everyone knew that Quinn, if he didn't actually kill Silverman, the fence, had at least directed the killing. Yet no one dared mention it. But he relaxed and smiled at the girl.

"You got guts," he nodded approval. "I should ring your neck for tossing out a crack like that, but I like it. So everyone knows that Senator Stone hands me orders? Does Mr. Strang know it?"

The girl said:

"Strang knows a lot. He must know that. You want something on Senator Stone? You want to be the real boss, eh?"

"Yes, I want something on him." Quinn set his lips tightly and his little eyes contracted to small black beads. "And that something is there too, Kid. It's in most big men's lives. A woman—graft—anything."

"You should know." The girl shrugged her shoulders.

"Try to find anything that's not connected with me." He put his hands upon her shoulders, pulled her close. "How about the Rolls and the penthouse, the jewelry and the furs?"

"No," she said, "while Stone's the big boss and Mr. Strang—lives."

"I'm the boss," said Quinn, "and Mr. Strang"—he pulled out his watch and looked at it—"is dead by now. You know that—you made the set-up. You'd have him at the Rosettie Restaurant."

The girl's eyes drifted to the clock on the wall. Her shoulders moved.

"Sure, and that should have convinced you I was still on the play for Strang, and that you didn't have to question me about his apartment."

"But you said you worked a trick to get him there. Walt phoned me when Strang went in."

"Strang went in!" The girl stared at the clock. "Why, it's only two thirty now. He wasn't to go until three. He couldn't have—"

"Yeah, yeah, I know." Martin Quinn tried to pull her a little closer without much success. "It's the boys, Wild Cat, they've been wondering about you—just some of them, understand. You set the stage for Steve Blake to kill Strang, and the thing blew up. Lester, of course, well, he got the dose. They just think you're hard luck."

The girl said:

"I don't understand what you mean."

"I mean," said Martin Quinn, "I had a dame buzz Mr. Strang's new address. She just left the message with his new servant, the Chink; setting the blow-out for an hour earlier. Killer Jackson wanted it that way and—" He held her close as she slumped against his body. He had to hold her too for her knees gave slightly.

MARTIN QUINN RUBBED his hand through her hair, patted her back. She tore herself from him, jumped back, both her hands behind her, clutching at the desk.

"Hell, Sweetheart." He stopped, and then: "What came over you?"

"There's time yet," the girl cried out shrilly. "Call Rosettie's, get Strang on the phone and—and—"

Martin Quinn's eyes were wide with surprise, uncertainty—and there was a spark of suspicion in them. But the phone rang. The one upon his desk. It rang sharply, twice, then insistently.

The girl's eyes watched him as he turned. Then she gripped the desk tightly, straightened herself. She was glad that Quinn's back was turned, for she found it hard walking to the water cooler, harder still holding the cup beneath the tiny stream.

It was the message, all right. She nodded. Strang was dead then and she had arranged it. All her plans, her clever plans, had failed. Strang was dead and— She took another drink of water, tried to pull herself together.

She gripped her bag tightly. There was a gun in it. But she'd never really get it out—never really pull the trigger. It wasn't because she was afraid to murder a man, if the killing of Martin Quinn could be called that. It was simply that her frozen fingers would not obey the message from her brain.

Quinn was turning his head. Resa Kent straightened her small body. She could at least face it out for him—for Strang. She could carry on where he left off. His vengeance would be her vengeance; his hate her hate. Some day her fingers would not be stiff and cold and uselessly frozen to the outside of her bag. She looked straight at Quinn. Her lips moved; formed words that were not heard. But those words were loud to her—pounded in her ears. The words of the man she had loved—still loved. Those words were: "Correct the Parole Evil."

But Quinn would know; surely he would read the horror of the thing she had done on her face. Her eyes widened. Quinn's face was white. His lips moved too—moved as he put the phone back in its prongs. But his words were clear to her. They were:

"Chief Inspector Barton just shot Killer Jackson to death—and Mr. Strang walked easily from the room. Why, what's the matter?"

And there was something the matter. Resa Kent, who had held herself together to hear of the death of Strang, now shrieked. A sudden, piercing almost hysterical scream before her own hand shot across her mouth and stopped it. She knew that she turned from Quinn and dashed to the far corner of the room. That her hand was still across her mouth; that the hysterical fear was suddenly gone. And she wanted to shout with joy!

Then she was herself, her brain working fast. She could see the doubt in Quinn's eyes. Again the quick-forming suspicion, and she bent every effort to stop it.

"So you fixed things," she shot the words through her teeth now like an infuriated woman. "You moved up the time an hour, because you didn't trust me. Because that two-timing cop, Cooper, put it into your head. Because Lester and Steve Blake couldn't face it when the time came to kill. And you want to know what's the matter!" She pounded at her little chest with both her hands, her bag knocking against her shoulder. "Well, he's alive. Alive because you didn't—wouldn't trust me."

QUINN'S SURPRISED LOOK faded. He was no longer amused. He walked straight to the girl—gripped her shoulders much as he had gripped Cooper's a short while before.

"Well," he demanded, "what's the beef? You said he'd be

there for an hour before Jackson came in. I thought he was
there to meet you—and you came here. What happened?"

The girl's knees gave beneath the pain of those fingers.
Then she straightened; upper teeth sank into a lower lip.
Water came out of her eyes. The pain almost turned her
stomach. She started to speak—failed—tried again. Quinn
loosened his fingers. The girl said:

"You know I lost my play with Strang. I got him there
this time because I promised him something and because—
well, because Chief Inspector Barton was to be there—was
to meet him there." The girl lied easily—without hesitation and in a convincing manner. It was her big moment
to settle herself firmly with Martin Quinn. She didn't for
a moment believe that Quinn had let Jackson hurry things
just because Jackson wanted to. And she knew that people
whom Quinn suspected just died. She lived then because
of the Rolls and the penthouse that Quinn wanted to give
her. But she went on:

"I had fixed it for Barton to leave at a certain time. I was
sure of that. And when he left there would be a good ten
minutes leeway for Jackson to do his stuff. Well—I named
the spot—put Strang on it—marked the time. So how do
I fit into this? Where did I slip this time?"

"Why—" Quinn found a pencil and juggled it. "I don't
know, Resa. But the lads have been talking. I've even got to
check up on myself at times." He gave a little gurgle that
sounded like a laugh. "Why don't you just quit it—you
know, be a girl that plays."

"You play too rough," she laughed unpleasantly. "And
you play with too many rats. They can't kill Strang. They

haven't got the stomach for it. They've got to shoot a man in the back and—"

Quinn cut in:

"There was never a better man than Steve Blake, nor a faster and quicker one than Johnny Lester. As for Jackson—Killer Jackson—he was half mad, you know, and we would have had to handle him later. This Strang bears a charmed life. I'm beginning to think you're right. He needs a bullet in the back." He grinned now as he hunted through his vest, found a thick cigar and lighted it. "The boys are getting too chivalrous, Kid. They must have been going to the movies." He stuck a match to the end of his Havana, took a few deep draws, looked long and carefully at the forming ash; finally said:

"All right, Sweetheart, run along now. Barton will be coming in to see me. At least he must have been surprised to see Jackson again."

Resa Kent said slowly:

"There's a matter of ten grand, Martin." And as Quinn started talking of Rolls and penthouses, "This is a matter of business, none of that playgirl stuff. It was to be ten G's to lay him on the spot. Ten G's."

"But he—well, nothing came of it."

"Ten grand, Martin." The girl stuck it out. "And I want it now. You're a guy who always lays it on the line; at least that's your line."

Quinn looked at her for a long time. He smiled as his teeth clamped down on the cigar. The girl wouldn't face him like that—bait him like that if—if— He dug a hand into his pocket, drew out a great roll of bills.

"Pin money, Kid," he said as he tossed it to her.

The girl counted it—eighteen hundred and twenty dollars.

"Welcher," she smiled back at him. There was no anger in her voice, however.

She had put her bluff across, she thought. But she couldn't see Quinn's round little eyes as she left the office— nor his twisted mouth as he sat drumming on the table.

Quinn frowned. There was Blutcher over at headquarters who had a very sick kid; needed money too. But he was dumber than hell, though some would call it honesty. Then there was Lieutenant Clode. That was the boy for him. There was a lad who knew his stuff, but he couldn't be touched with a hundred grand. He was a fool. But that young guy—that lad who had been snatched off his beat and put into headquarters. There was a boy with a head—a boy who'd get somewhere and wanted to get there quickly. A boy who liked money—liked it smack on the line and in a hurry. Yes, Quinn might do business with him.

For over half an hour Quinn smoked in silence. He was thinking of the girl. A sweet armful, of course, and she'd been straight with him. Still—well, a lad ought to know. Men who trusted women never got very far in life. The private phone rang.

Quinn said into the mouthpiece:

"Fine, Charlie!" A longer pause and then: "Squawked like a stuck pig, eh? Well, you never can tell."

This time when the phone clicked off Quinn did not sit down again. He lifted his cane and gloves and left the office. He was quite sure that Gertie Bender was not a girl to turn loose. She was too smart—knew too much. If women like Gertie would keep their noses out of men's business they wouldn't die so young. Gertie would never stand for Resa Kent. She'd shoot her face off all over the Avenue. Too bad—he had rather liked Gertie.

He thought of Charlie Devine and shook his head. Charlie would want a fortune for a female job. His shoulders moved up and down. It would have to be Harry Davidson again. He disliked using the same man, but, hell, there was nothing else to do about it. Gertie had to take the rap. He couldn't move Resa in without moving Gertie out—and he had set the stage long ago for Gertie's blow.

But he liked Charlie Devine. The best executioner in town. He never made mistakes; never kicked or grumbled about a job.

And Martin Quinn stopped right on the sidewalk. His lips parted and his little eyes shone brightly. He certainly was using his head this day, Mr. Strang—Charlie Devine— It was worth the money it would cost. Besides, as he saw it now, it would put the Senator right smack on the spot—an accessory to murder.

4

WHO IS MR. STRANG?

SIMON BECKER, WHO for years had gone unnoticed in the underworld except for small transactions that took place in the room behind his little pawn shop, rubbed his hands, bent his old shoulders, blinked his eyes at Mr. Strang.

Strang faced him, reciting slowly the advantages that he, Strang, had given Simon over the few years of their acquaintance. His words were a simple monotone. He was saying:

"You knew nothing but poverty. I paid you to get me information about Quinn. Simon, you were the forgotten man of crime, forgotten even by the police. You were but stuffed furniture who sat silent and ignored in the presence of desperate men. Silverman was Quinn's fence. Now you whom Quinn trusted—Silverman who finally gave you stuff to handle—are Quinn's fence. Everything that has come to you has come through me." Strang looked up suddenly. "Quinn deals with you personally now?"

Simon nodded.

"That is right. Quinn's lieutenants have been killed. He does not suspect that you come here. He fears you, for he has warned me that you may discover me as you discovered Silverman—kill me as you killed Silverman."

Strang smiled inwardly. So Martin Quinn did not take the credit for that killing; the brutal murder of an old man. Strang rather liked the credit for that kill. It gave him a stronger grip on Simon Becker.

"Well," Mr. Strang said after a long pause, "you gave me the evidence. I have looked it over carefully. You have done well, Simon." Strang put the papers in his pocket. There was enough there to roast Quinn over and over. Strang frowned. He said finally:

"What of Senator Stone? There is nothing in this carefully written paper that can touch him."

Simon Becker said:

"There is nothing that one can connect directly to Senator Stone. He is a very clever man. I know nothing of him, except what Martin Quinn has let it slip out many times—that Stone is the big influence." He clutched Strang by the arm. "Those papers—I am making more money in a month than I made in years. What are you going to do with them? You have made me Quinn's man. What money you wish is yours. You—it is not a simple vengeance. You are not going to expose Quinn to the police?"

"No," Strang said. "And the money you make, you may keep—all of it."

"All of it! All of it!" Simon's eyes shone. His tongue came out and licked at dead, yellow lips. "All that Quinn gives me for moving his stuff, for finding agents in other states; other countries even? All that Quinn allows me? And you want nothing?"

"I want," said Strang very slowly, "Quinn's job. I want to

be the man next to Stone. This evidence shown to Senator Stone should give that job to me."

"But me—me—" Simon's words stuck in his throat. Fear held them there and fear finally gasped them out. "Mr. Quinn will kill me. I will be dead the very moment after the Senator speaks to him. You have Quinn's record there; his past. You must see. You must understand. A hundred murders directly at his door."

Simon Becker clung desperately to Strang now, tried to thrust his hand into his pocket to recover the written sheets that would send Martin Quinn to the chair and himself a riddled mass of old flesh, in some gutter.

STRANG BRUSHED THE old man's hand aside as he said:

"My life then would also be in danger. So you may be sure that Quinn will be dead before I take his place." After a moment, "Your report is good, especially the part I wanted so badly. Those murders of years back when Judge Robert T. Kenyon and his friend, Kenneth Hastings, the District Attorney down in Green County, were so ruthlessly shot to death. You are sure that Quinn obtained the parole of those two murderers for the express purpose of killing Judge Kenyon and the District Attorney?"

"Absolutely positive." Simon Becker looked surprised. "I traced that killing straight to Quinn. It was done with his orders. He sat there, far back in the darkness of a car when it was done. He directed it. It is common knowledge of the underworld, but not evidence that could convict him in court. But it happened many years ago. Why is it important now?"

"Why?" Strang straightened. Blue veins stood out on his forehead. "Because that murder aroused for a while the entire country, and though the actual killers have since died the man who directed their minds, their hand, their guns still lives. The people of the state await justice."

Simon Becker said:

"The people have forgotten as they always forget."

Strang's eyes burned when he spoke.

"But one person could not have forgotten. The murdered judge led a little boy by the hand. A little boy who looked into that car and recognized the third man. That third man was never tried because that little boy never came to court and testified against him. But the boy identified his picture as Martin Quinn. Quinn, who was a young man then. Quinn, who was just starting to rule. Quinn, whose career would have been ended by Judge Kenyon and the District Attorney if they had not died."

"Yes, yes," Simon agreed. "It is in the papers there. But now it is all forgotten."

"Not by the little boy who was shot in the head. Not by the little boy whom surgeons refused to operate on, for that bullet was imbedded in his brain. Not by that little boy who was smuggled off to Paris because of the threats of death if he testified. That little boy who couldn't play with other little boys because he never thought of life, only of death. That boy, Robert Kenyon, grew to manhood and, though assured by great surgeons that the operation to remove the bullet would be simple, insisted that the bullet remain there. He left it there, Simon, because he feared that he might think of life again if it was removed. Left it there because he had betrayed his father, his father's friend, and the family of his father's friend." Strang paused, then said slowly, "Yes, that little boy when he grew to be a man sent a letter every month to the widow of the District Attorney, Mrs. Kenneth Hastings, and that letter promised—Vengeance."

"Vengeance against Martin Quinn?"

"Yes, in the beginning. Then—" Mr. Strang shook his head. In another moment he would have told the truth. As the years went on he had brooded and hated more. He read of the deaths of others; of children who had been made fatherless by criminals on parole. His vengeance became broader. It became a vengeance against a system instead of a man—a rotten, foul system. Vengeance against the evil of parole and the man who controlled it. And that man was Martin Quinn.

SIMON TRIED TO speak, but no words came. He had always feared Mr. Strang and knew, as he always knew, that this man, in anger, was a greater danger than any man he had ever faced in the underworld; and he had faced many. At last he did speak, not the words he wanted to speak, for he knew the answer to the question without asking it. But just the same he heard the words issuing from his mouth even as Strang turned to the door. Those words were:

"You—you were that little boy?"

Mr. Strang turned, said:

"Correct. I was that little boy." He placed his hand upon the knob of the door that gave to the little steps, the yard behind, and the vacant house through which he would seek the street beyond. Then he swung back suddenly, walked slowly to Simon Becker.

"Simon," he said, and he did not raise his voice. "One word of this to anyone—one word to Martin Quinn and I will return and empty my gun into your body."

There was no menace in the speech; nothing of the melodramatic about the words themselves. Yet to Simon Becker they were more sinister and terrifying than if Mr. Strang had shouted the words as he held a gun against Simon's head.

For a long moment Mr. Strang looked directly into Simon's eyes. He didn't speak again. He simply walked to the door, opened it carefully and closed it behind him.

Then Simon Becker found his voice.

"God in Heaven!" he cried aloud. "Martin Quinn only plays with death! Compared with—with Mr. Strang—"

And a voice spoke behind Simon Becker, a voice from the heavy door that led to the shop. The voice said:

"Really, Mr. Becker, I should have come earlier and heard what the man had to say. But then Mr. Strang has always had the happy faculty of leaving places when I come in. However, he is going straight to his death. Now, Mr. Becker, tell me just what Mr. Strang said. Tell me—"

Simon Becker started to his feet with a shriek of terror. But he never reached his feet. Martin Quinn's huge bulk moved with the speed of a mountain lion. Great arms shot forward. Strong fingers stretched out and Simon's scream gurgled to silence in his throat.

It was Martin Quinn who carefully lifted the unconscious Simon Becker into an old chair. It was Martin Quinn who gently poured the brandy down Simon Becker's throat and patted him on the back when he choked. He watched Simon's eyes open, watched the color start creeping back into that wrinkled face—to disappear the very second his blinking eyes rested on the face of Martin Quinn.

"Come, come, Simon," Martin said softly. "I'm not blaming you. After all, you didn't betray me. It was Strang who paid you in the beginning. That's how it was—eh, Simon? Sure, got to stick to the lad who hired you. That's loyalty. That's how it was, wasn't it?"

Simon's eyes bulged more than Quinn's.

"That's how it was," he spoke at last.

"Sure, sure." Quinn nodded, played with the head of his cane between his knees. He had searched Simon Becker carefully while he was unconscious. "But if you want to live; Simon, you've got to come to my side of the fence."

Simon's eyes blinked. He stammered:

"You'd kill me anyway—kill me, and for the first time in my life I'm in the big money."

Quinn shook his head.

"No. It's like this, Simon—I need you. But I've got to trust you. Exactly who is Mr. Strang?"

SIMON GULPED AND told him. Went through the whole story, said:

"He's Judge Robert Kenyon's boy. He's come back for vengeance."

Quinn's eyes grew so wide that there seemed to be no lids, just bulging balls beneath heavy eyebrows. But his voice showed no emotion.

"I knew it," he said. "That is, I knew there was something back of it, and I should have—" He paused. "But that was years ago." And suddenly leaning forward, "He wanted you to betray me, of course, to search into my past. Don't you see, Simon, he's with the law. He's the man who has tipped off Barton—raised him from a forgotten Police Lieutenant to Chief Inspector. Why he's made a fool of you!"

"But he wanted your place—wanted to be the man next to Stone. He—" Simon Becker stopped. He didn't want to say too much.

"That's what he fed you." Quinn nodded. He got up, patted Simon on the shoulder, said, "Well, did you put the finger on me for him?"

"Not much—not much." Simon's fear came back again. That is, if it had ever gone. Then he saw his chance and he took it. It was only through him that Quinn could be saved. He told Quinn that he had discovered nothing about the Senator.

"So he was interested in Senator Stone too?" Martin Quinn rubbed his chins. He pulled up a chair and talked to Simon, talked to him as an equal, talked to him as one big shot to another. Simon liked it. Quinn's promises sounded good. So good that Becker not only lost his fear, but began to take advantage of it. Becker said:

"It's this filthy place. You insisted—yes, demanded that I stay here. Yet Silverman lived like a prince, surrounded by luxury. I am as big a man as he was now."

"Well—" Quinn pulled down his lower lip. "You've always lived like this. I didn't want the police to take an interest in you through sudden affluence. I tell you, Simon. We might locate a forgotten daughter, a wealthy one. You might live with her."

Simon's tongue licked at his lips, his eyes rolled. His bones showed through worn skin when he spoke.

"She might be like some of Silverman's friends, eh? Young, nice—I have money now and I will have much more."

"Sure, why not, Simon? Enjoy life when you can. I've

always been free and easy with the boys." Quinn lifted up his cane, stood up. "There wasn't anything written you might have given Mr. Strang? Anything that would come back on you as well as me?"

Simon hesitated. There were quick flashes in his brain. If Mr. Strang was with the law he, as well as Quinn, was through. If Mr. Quinn was jailed he was also through. He, Simon, must get that paper—those pages of paper about Quinn. They must be recovered. Simon Becker didn't like it, but he had to talk.

"There is something—something I had to do. I was working for Mr. Strang, you know. It is to your interest to know—your interest to recover something." And as those beady eyes rested on him, "It won't—you won't—"

MARTIN QUINN'S LIDS closed to narrow slits. Tiny pointed dots of black showed through fishlike film. He said:

"If he has something in writing, Simon, you'd better speak quickly. If—" And seeing the sudden fear beginning to return to Simon's eyes he realized that his voice had changed. He spoke softly, earnestly, sincerely. "Tell me, Simon. I give you my word, the sacred word of Martin Quinn, which has never been broken, that I will not harm you. I only want to help you—the word of Martin Quinn."

And Simon told him about the many written sheets which he had given to Mr. Strang. He had to tell him. If Quinn got them from Strang it wouldn't matter. But he didn't like Quinn's eyes nor the way his face hardened as he spoke.

Martin Quinn walked quietly to the door, opened it and looked out into the deserted shop. Then he closed the door and as he walked across the room to the rear exit said to Simon:

"I had a key to your place made for me. Just to surprise you." He spun the key in the rear door and opening it looked toward the vacant house in the rear. Then he locked the door and came back to Simon. He said:

"Mr. Strang left here to go straight to his death. He went to Senator Stone."

"But surely he'll hide those sheets some place first."

"No," said Quinn. "He won't have the time—and if he did you won't have anything to worry about. Not a thing, Simon."

Almost casually Martin Quinn laid his cane against the wall. Then he drew a heavy forty-five from beneath his left armpit. Without another word he shot Simon Becker. Shot him five times in the stomach. He lifted his cane, took his gloves from his pocket, passed through the rear door, and walked hurriedly to the street behind.

Quinn was slightly worried. Not so much that Strang would use that evidence against him, at least not until he was sure of Senator Stone. His greatest danger was that Strang might actually show that evidence to Stone and—

But Martin Quinn shook his head. Charlie never failed, and he would get those papers when he searched the body of Mr. Strang which the freshly painted laundry wagon would bring to him. That would be any time now. He'd better get moving.

But Martin Quinn was not smiling. Mr. Strang was a dangerous man. He had put Quinn in a position where Quinn found it necessary to kill both of his receivers and distributors of stolen goods. Yes, the best two fences in the city. Silverman first and now Becker.

And Strang himself had shot to death few men, very few men, that Quinn had trusted. Now, well, Quinn had dealt directly with Simon Becker and look what happened. Martin Quinn smiled then—a nasty smile.

5

THE EXECUTIONER

SENATOR ROBERT CARSON STONE set his glasses more firmly upon his nose. Twice he walked to the long curtains some ten feet behind his desk and spoke to the man who stood quietly there.

"Mr. Quinn has recommended you highly," he repeated for the third time. "I'm quite sure there will be no trouble here in my house. I'm rather doubtful if he'll come."

"If it's Mr. Strang, and he accepted the appointment, he will come." The grim-faced man looked from Senator Stone down to the long, black-barreled revolver in his right hand. "And you have nothing to worry about. He'll never start any trouble. Just a poke of his nose through these curtains—and you're safe."

Senator Stone looked at his flat desk—a comfortable chair on either side of it. He thought aloud.

"Now if he sits with his back to you, you can't be sure just what he intends to do. If he face you, why—"

"Through the back of a man's head is always the safest. I'll guess what he's going to do, and whatever it is he won't do it."

"Ah, but that's it. I know he's a bad man. I know he's a very dangerous man. I am going to threaten him to leave the city—the state even. He's been drawing the attention of the papers to me in a most unpleasant manner. But I don't want him—" He looked at that hard, cruel face. "I don't want him killed here."

"Better you than him," said Charlie Devine. "Mr. Quinn wouldn't let anything happen to you, Senator. I—" He stopped. Charlie was Quinn's ace executioner. His orders were to kill Mr. Strang and to shoot him to death in the Senator's house. Charlie never bothered to think about the reason for the kill. He left that for others. But he liked to set his own stage.

It was the first time Charlie had ever stood face to face with the great Senator Stone, the man whom everyone in the know on the Avenue knew backed Quinn. And if it weren't for that knowledge Charlie would have taken him for just what he pretended to be—a pompous, open-handed, open-hearted friend of the people. A politician of the old school who had beamed his way up with pious, cheery thoughts. Yet he had orders from Martin Quinn to shoot Mr. Strang in that house—and, despite Senator Stone's objections, he would do just that.

Senator Stone was arranging the wide, black ribbon that ran down from his nose-glasses to be lost somewhere in the vest across his ample stomach.

"Shoot only as a last resort," he admonished Charlie with a raised finger. "You know if he draws a gun you're to shoot it out of his hand—out of his hand, understand?"

Charlie smiled. He thought the Senator had seen too many movies, or perhaps behind that florid face the Senator was having his little joke. He could just imagine himself shooting a gun out of Mr. Strang's hand.

"Sure, Senator," he agreed. "I understand." And he thought he did. For he had seen the newly-painted delivery wagon on the street behind the Senator's house and read the letters "Madison's Laundry—Twenty-Four Hour Service." Sure he understood. The Senator was one of these birds who talked like that before a kill. Well, he'd make his first shot blast a hole straight through Mr. Strang's head. He had seen too many of the boys down at the morgue with Mr. Strang's bullets in them. Mr. Strang not only shot to kill, he did kill. Just one thing Charlie was determined on. Mr. Strang was not going to shoot at all. When the Senator waited, Charlie said:

"You want to talk to him a bit first, eh?"

Don't be a fool!" The Senator removed his glasses now and tapped them on the palm of his hand. "Of course, I want to talk to him. That's why I'm having him here. That's why I'm having you here. That's why I'm apparently alone in the house—" He moved to the desk, placed the heavy revolver on the opposite side. He had decided to let Mr. Strang face the curtain.

The front door bell was ringing.

Charlie said simply:

"Don't worry, Senator," and he slipped behind the curtain. A practiced hand straightened them, held them from waving. Then the long-nosed revolver came up, picked out the split in the curtain, forced its way gently between the slits and remained there—steady—still— unmoving—unseen from outside. Charlie was just a bit proud of his work. He was a bit cocky, too. Now he waited patiently. Patience was Charlie's greatest virtue. It was men who hurried these things who failed. Charlie never failed. He was alive to prove that. He listened to the feet of the Senator going down the stairs, and heard, too, the bell ring again. He let his glance slip through the curtains and rest upon the clock. He was thinking of the ten grand for the knockover. It came easy—ten minutes for the job and someone else would handle the body.

WHEN MR. STRANG left Simon Becker he felt the temptation to take those papers straight to Barton. But he didn't do that. He had not thought that the evidence would be so complete, but he had hoped it would not only involve, but actually send Senator Stone to the chair. Therefore, going over the papers had kept him much longer than he had expected to stay with Simon Becker.

He couldn't be late for his present appointment—and he couldn't expose Quinn yet. That would be a personal vengeance—the vengeance of which he wrote to Mrs. Kenneth Hastings, wife of the district attorney. For a long time now he had considered himself simply the head of a mission—a mission to destroy the present vicious Parole System. To destroy those who let loose in the great city the jackals of the night—the paroled convicts who went forth to kill again.

Just one thought as he reached the house of Senator Robert Carson Stone and climbed the huge, stone steps to the thick front door. He hoped he wasn't mad and that he would live just long enough to finish his last letter to Mrs. Hastings. Each letter that he wrote caused him to relive again the murder of his father and his father's friend; to see plainly Martin Quinn far back in that cab of death. Yes, when he wrote he actually saw those brutal murders; even heard the crash of the shots. He could still hear the last death cry of his father as he gripped the hand of a small boy who was his son.

Senator Robert Carson Stone opened the big front door and stood back as Mr. Strang entered. His voice was cheery.

"You are a business man, sir. I suppose you thought I invited you here this evening to discuss purchasing pictures?"

"No." Strang turned half sideways from the light. "I did not think you invited me here for that purpose. I'm a blunt man, Senator. You have invited me here to warn me."

"Oh, come, come, Mr. Strang—for I know you are known as Mr. Strang as well as Strang Cummings. You—you—"

Senator Stone sucked in a great breath, rocked partly back on his heels. For a moment he thought that he was looking at a living dead man. Sunken cheeks—sunken eyes, with the fires of hell raging in them.

Senator Stone restrained an involuntary shudder, said something about Strang leaving his topcoat on the chair. He turned his head to avoid those eyes and, recovering somewhat, said:

"To warn you, eh? To warn you not to interfere with the business of the state—is that it?"

"No," said Strang, "that is not it. To warn me of death—sudden and violent death."

"Oh, come, come now." This was hardly the reply the Senator had expected. "Let us go up to my study and talk."

"After you, Senator." Mr. Strang stood aside to let the Senator precede him up the stairs.

THE SENATOR COUGHED and started up the stairs. His right hand held firmly to the banister.

"If you have such thoughts about me, it's a wonder you have come alone to my house." And when there was no answer he asked, "Aren't you afraid?"

"No," said Mr. Strang.

"You don't fear death, then?"

"Not if my mission is completed first."

"But—er—you do not fear death here tonight before your—this mission you speak of is completed?"

"Tonight, if I should die, my mission would first be completed. The man who controls a great evil would not be alive to further control it."

"Good God!" Senator Stone turned and faced Strang. "What do you mean by that?"

"Exactly what you think I mean."

The Senator turned and walked quickly up the rest of the stairs, turned left at the landing and went straight to his study. This man was mad all right. He was sorry now that he had asked the man there at all. But he thought of the man behind the curtains and realized it would be safer to go through with the talk than to try to back out of it now, even if it were possible to back out of it.

Senator Stone walked quickly into his study, shot one rapid glance at the curtains. Then the curtains moved ever so slightly. Senator Stone breathed deeply and looked at Mr. Strang. Mr. Strang's sharp eyes were covering that entire room.

If Senator Stone still planned to place Strang in the chair facing the curtains it did not matter now. Mr. Strang had maneuvered into that position. They both sat down together, and Mr. Strang was facing the curtains behind the Senator.

Senator Stone moved his chair slightly so as to give Charlie a better view of Mr. Strang. Mr. Strang moved with him, and as he moved his eyes settled on the gun upon the desk. But this glance seemed one of idle curiosity. He made no attempt to touch that gun; just sat far forward and stared straight at the Senator. Both Mr. Strang's hands rested on the desk. His long, strong fingers showed white against it.

Senator Stone cleared his throat and said, "Just a simple precaution, you know. I hope you do not mind the gun?"

Maybe Strang's words should have assured Senator Stone, but they certainly did not. Strang said:

"Not at all. Indeed, Senator, I would not mind if you attempted to use it."

"No—no." The Senator looked at the gun again. It was very close to his right hand. The Senator coughed, stiffened and got down to business.

"You are," Senator Stone said, "against parole—or so you claim. But I am told that, after all, you are out for but one person—yourself. Your killings, at least the few openly investigated by the police, proved self-defense. In plain words, Mr. Strang, I've brought you here tonight to warn you privately. You are interfering with my work to correct the Parole System of this state. It is not parole itself that is at fault, but the method of administering it."

MR. STRANG SMILED and said: "Administering it as it was administered with a murderer called Jackson, Killer Jackson, released without notice being given to the papers or to the police? He was shot to death by Chief Inspector Barton."

"That, of course, was an unfortunate mistake." Stone

leaned forward and his voice was low. "The Parole Board has been releasing men on the average of fifty a day for the past month."

"Yes?" Mr. Strang straightened. That was something he did not know. He was sure that Barton did not know that either.

"They were released through my suggestion after a long talk with the Governor, who is my friend. I want you to know the dangerous ground and the tender feet you are treading on with some of your outlandish letters to the papers and your one-man law enforcement."

"So you're turning them loose and admit it," Mr. Strang said. "And you tell me; tell the man who wants the world to know it. You must be very sure of yourself, Senator—far too sure."

"I am telling you because you must leave the state tonight. I am telling you because even your sincerity has been forced upon me. I am telling you because you are a menace to the new Parole Law I hope to force through the Legislature to safeguard the people. And I am telling you because you would find out—as the papers must find out—and misinterpret the reason for these men being turned loose."

"So you have a reason for this wholesale release of desperate men?"

"I have," said the Senator. "It is a simple reason. I have made a study of the penal system of other states as well as ours, and I have found that the greatest menace to prison life—the greatest obstacle in the way of reform, the rehabilitation of these men—is the overcrowding of our prisons. There is the State Penitentiary. It has accommodations, and not too generous accommodations for fifteen hundred men. Today, despite the fact that fifty a day are being turned loose, that prison holds three thousand, eight hundred men. Think of it! Four in one cell, and many more in these years being admitted every day. Young men, boys, middle-aged men, who in the grip of an agonizing depression, fall into temptation and commit crimes. Is it any wonder that, a few years later, honest men—at least men who wanted to be honest—come out of prison fully developed criminals?"

Strang looked at the man. He was a liar, of course. That was not his reason, but certainly he was convincing. "What's the answer?"

"The answer," said Senator Stone, "is more prisons—at once. The prevention of crime, rather than the punishment of it. A Parole Administration that must rely on the man's former record rather than the recommendation of certain wardens who get their information from guards whose salaries are so small that they are subject to corruption by the characters of the underworld."

Strang's mouth hung open. He could see now why Barton was fooled; why the Governor might have been fooled, and he could see how one man might easily get control of the entire Parole System. And that one man, Senator Stone, the friend of the people, the friend of the Governor, and the *Friend of Martin Quinn*. The racket, then, was not dying down. It was getting worse. Much worse if Stone could gain such control; Stone of the kindly eyes, the placid face, the even, white, friendly teeth. The man who— And Strang raised his head.

THE SENATOR WAS talking again. He was saying:

"Of course, under the circumstances, because of the room

needed to receive the newcomers, it is not just the model prisoners who are released on parole. At times, perhaps, we must release just the least vicious. Martin Quinn has advised me. He has been very helpful. He admits quite freely that his environment at one time was such that he might very easily—indeed to a certain extent did—enter a life of crime. Today he has made a success that many a less honest man in business might be proud of."

Senator Stone stopped talking. He saw those eyes before him burning now—lighting up with the fires of hell. Mr. Strang's right hand was creeping up his vest along his chest across to the left armpit. A left armpit from which the jacket fell back and black showed—hard, square black, the grip of a heavy thirty-eight revolver.

Senator Robert Carson Stone saw something else in those eyes, the slowly moving hand. He saw death—death for himself. He tried to cry out and couldn't.

Senator Stone was a big man; he faced big situations. He was facing one now. Maybe he lost his head—maybe he didn't. Maybe it was the sudden physical courage of a man who seldom had occasion to use it. But he did cry out as he leaned forward over his desk and grasped frantically for that gun.

Yet as his fingers gripped its cold surface, his eyes remained fastened upon Strang. He didn't actually see the hand any more. Only the white flash of it. He couldn't tell if that hand went beneath Strang's armpit or not. But it must have. Because the hand that was white now held something black and shiny.

Senator Stone turned up his hand; started to close his finger upon the trigger. He saw the black flash before him;

he felt the pound of something heavy across the top of his head—almost the very second that he heard the gun roar. A gun that seemed to explode right into his head. For a moment there was the smell of burnt powder in his nostrils. Then the gun dropped limply from his fingers and thudded upon the desk.

Stone's body swung; his eyes were blurred. But he saw the curtains where Charlie hid. Saw them part. Saw Charlie pitch forward on his face.

There was blood running down Senator Stone's face, into his eyes, yet in a dim way he knew what had happened. Mr. Strang had lunged suddenly across that desk and crashed a gun down upon his head—crashed it down almost the very moment that Mr. Strang's finger closed upon the trigger and shot Charlie Devine to death.

Senator Stone gripped tightly to the arms of the chair. He felt himself going even before he toppled from the chair. And just before he sank to the floor he heard Mr. Strang speak, heard his words distinctly. And those words were:

"Charlie Devine, eh? Martin Quinn's star executioner—and he never even closed a finger upon his gun trigger."

After that just blackness for Senator Robert Carson Stone.

6

MURDER AND MADNESS

MR. STRANG CAME very slowly to his feet, stood for a moment looking at the gun upon the desk, walked to curtains and swung them open, stepping over the dead Devine on the floor without even a glance. He went to the closet, looked in. He walked to the hall door, listened, felt the papers in his pocket and looked down at Senator Stone. For a moment he stood beside him, his gun dangling in his hand, contemplating the gray hair now matted with the blood. As he looked he thought: Senator Stone is fairly young and would have many more years of political activity. He was a friend of the Governor. He was in a fair way to control the Parole System of the state. Clever that. He could be the power behind it without being of it. The lives of men, women and children would be in his hands. Good honest American citizens who some day would be shot down upon the public streets by criminals freed by this man.

Strang's shoulders moved restlessly. The papers in his pocket would wipe Martin Quinn out. But what was the good of that if Senator Robert Carson Stone, the real leader, still lived?

But what did he have that would actually end Stone?

Nothing—absolutely nothing. Nothing? Mr. Strang looked again at the unconscious Senator, and his glance ran off the end of his own gun. His eyes burned with a new brilliancy. If he had in his pocket papers that would wipe out Quinn, he had in his right hand the thing that would forever wipe out Senator Robert Carson Stone—just as effectively as it had wiped out Charlie Devine. Charlie Devine could be replaced by a thousand other men, but Senator Stone could never be replaced.

Strang moved his gun slightly; just a sure twist of his wrist; the movement he had practiced ever since he was a boy. His arm stiffened. His whole body straightened. His lips became a single red gash.

Strang hadn't missed when he shot Killer Jackson. Strang hadn't missed when he shot Charlie Devine. He knew he wouldn't miss then. Now he looked down at the unconscious man. He couldn't miss. Just the slightest pressure of a finger, just the single roar of a gun, just the tiny, blue hole that would widen and turn red, and—

Murder! The cold-blooded murder of a helpless man. Yes, he thought of that. His eyes burned. His lips parted. He was going to kill a helpless, unconscious man. He stepped over the body—bent low—drew a bead right between those eyes. He was mad; yes, mad and he didn't care. The madness that he had feared was upon him and he didn't fear it now. He gloried in it. He was lost to everything else but death. His finger tightened upon the trigger.

A body struck against him. An arm hit against his arm as his gun roared. But the bullet from that gun pounded into the wood of the floor a good six inches from the unconscious man's head.

Strang turned and swept the girl from him.

"Resa—Resa Kent," he said, and then, "Get out; get out! Can't you see—can't you understand! This is the man."

And she was at him again. Her little chest almost flat against the gun he held in his hand; her arms about his neck, her hair brushing his cheek.

"Strang, Strang," she cried over and over. "Don't you understand it would be murder? No! No!" She tore at the hands that pushed her away. "You're not sure. You're not—"

HE HELD HER from him, looked into her brown eyes; looked at them a long time. He saw the honest clearness, the great depths that had made him believe in her even when he thought she was betraying him. He finally said:

"It doesn't matter, Resa. It doesn't matter about me. Look at me. Can't you see—don't you understand? It's happened. I'm mad—yes, I'm mad."

"Nonsense." She spoke very calmly, but the hands that held his trembled. "You're wrapped up in an obsession, that's all. You'll clear it up. You said it could be done by a slight operation."

"I lied about it being slight." He looked straight at her. "And the bullet is there, eating away my brain." Strang looked down at Stone. "He is alive tonight. Tomorrow, if I let him live, I may be dead."

He stopped—his hand left her shoulder. She wanted him to keep talking. Was it to save him from killing Senator Stone? Or to save Senator Stone from being killed by him? She didn't give ground when he released her. She shot suddenly forward, held him again.

"Strang," she said, "I love you. Don't do this. I love you."

The man's eyes still burned with fires of hate, but the fire of madness was going very slowly.

This time he held her head as he pushed it back and looked at her.

"I'm sorry, Resa," he said. "Sorry that I cannot—dare not find any love in my body." And, suddenly, "You sent me to a restaurant. As a man, I trusted you. As a mission, I didn't. And through that distrust—through a gun held beneath my napkin during the entire time I was there—my life was saved. Can you explain that?"

"Yes," she said slowly. "I can explain that."

"Explain it."

"No," she said. "Do you trust me now?"

His laugh was like a shovel across a cellar floor. He did not answer. He thought he did not need to. But the girl's eyes held his. He finally said again:

"Explain it."

She shook her head.

"Not until you answer me. Without an explanation do you believe in me?" And this time her eyes held his so steadily that he did not laugh. He just looked at her, shook his head, but his eyes remained fixed. But he said:

"Yes, God help me, I trust and believe in you."

She tried to make her laugh easy, her words light, but failed miserably.

"Such is the strength of woman," she laughed. Then her head was on his shoulder. She was sobbing softly. Such was the weakness of woman, but neither the man nor the girl thought of that then. After a while she straightened, daubed at her eyes, said:

"It's the first time I have cried in years. You're not going to kill him, Strang. You can't—not like that."

He looked down at Stone.

"No," he said, "I'm not going to kill him—like that." But there was no remorse in his voice, only bitterness.

"And you are not going to ask what happened today? Nor how I happened to be here?"

"No," he said, "I am not."

"I am here because I have worked for Senator Stone lately—obtained the position through Quinn or Quinn's influence. So I have a key to the door."

"Stone gave you a key?"

"I simply said that I have a key. I wanted to find information against Stone. Quinn wished it. He wishes to hold something over him."

"Then you know that Stone is the big man in the racket?"

"Yes," she nodded. "Quinn has admitted that."

Strang paced the floor, a frown creasing his forehead. Finally he spoke: "Is there a typewriter here?"

She pointed to a leather case close to the fireplace. Then followed Strang's instructions. She found paper, pushed it into the machine and typed rapidly as Strang dictated. It was a letter to Senator Stone. From the papers in his pocket Strang dictated much damning evidence against Quinn.

The girl finished, put the sheets together.

"Why?" she asked.

"I want Stone to know what I have on Quinn, and perhaps think I may also have plenty on him."

"He won't believe it," she said. "I mean about himself."

"But he may believe that Quinn, arrested, will talk. Talk

232 CARROLL JOHN DALY

when he thinks in the day and dreams in the night of burning flesh in the electric chair."

"Quinn must know about Stone, yet I doubt if he could prove anything. Certainly I could find no proof of a connection between them."

Strang said:

"If Stone is afraid or alarmed he will act in some way to protect Quinn. If he believes I have knowledge that will not only expose but convict him he will flee in panic. If he runs away, then I can turn these papers over to Inspector Barton and the racket will be over."

The notes were left carefully beside Senator Stone's now twitching fingers.

Strang led the girl from the room. He wondered where she fitted into the picture. He asked her, after she had insisted they leave by the cellar window, and they were safely a couple of blocks away.

"Resa," he said, "what brought you into this?"

She stopped him; a finger against his lips.

"First," she said, "because I hate where you hate. Second, because I met you and wished to help you. Third, because I like you and wish to save you. Fourth, because I love you desperately and want you—for myself."

But that was just before she suddenly ran towards a cruising taxi and disappeared.

7

A BROKEN MAN

CHIEF INSPECTOR JAMES BARTON, lifted his whisky, twirled it slightly, watched the oil form inside the glass, and carefully wiped it off with a huge forefinger. Then he added just a bit more water and drank it slowly.

Strang spoke.

"It's time for Resa Kent to telephone me."

"You've got a fine idea there," Barton told him. "Having her call you every night. You know she's safe then." He leaned forward. "Tell me more about the other night; the death of Charlie Devine at Senator Stone's house." And Barton watched Strang for that madness he had never seen in that face and which Strang feared so much.

Strang laughed. It was not such an unpleasant laugh this time—almost a human laugh, Barton thought.

"So you're thinking of the madness now," Strang said. "But I did go to the Senator's house. I cracked his skull when he would have used a gun. And I did shoot Charlie Devine to death. I've gone all through that before."

"And so have I." Barton got up and paced the room. "Senator Stone's was empty. There were no spots of blood on the rugs. No dead body of any kind, and the Senator himself has disappeared. His servants returned the next morning. His secretary can't locate him—just says he's out of town."

Barton stopped and twisted slightly. "And when I damn near drove that secretary's chest in with the heel of my hand he admitted that Senator Stone had telephoned him, said he was all right and would be away for a few days."

"Sure, sure—" Strang nodded grimly. "Can't I make you understand? Stone has taken a run-out powder. He came to after my blow, read my note, tidied up the room and fled. It proves him guilty. Don't you see? His call to his secretary was just a ruse. He's not sure. If nothing happens he'll come back."

"But why would he run away? Come, come, Strang. You've talked about a note. You've talked about papers that would convict Quinn. Yet you do not produce such documents. Look here—" Barton stood before Strang now. "You're sure everything happened as you said? Remember, you've had a shock. You told me that the murdered Simon Becker was your last link with the underworld. All right, admit Quinn rubbed Becker out. Who's to prove that before twelve men? Then there was Joe Cooper. I watched him day and night—had him too. Was just going to clamp down on him when he pops up with the top of his head blown off. How did Quinn know I wanted him? How did Quinn know you used Simon Becker?"

"Just the breaks," said Strang.

"The breaks, hell!" Barton slammed out the words. "I don't know if I'm in a hole or not. If I send out a general alarm for Stone I may stir up a hornets' nest. He might pop back and raise the devil. And he can raise hell in this state despite your suspicions of him. The Commissioner of Police is leaving everything to me now. He's far from a well man. He's had his resignation in for several months. I don't mind telling you that I've heard indirectly from the Mayor that I'll be the Commissioner, and damn soon too."

"So you've got to step right, eh?"

BARTON STRAIGHTENED.

"You know it's not that. It's your wild story. The rugs are clean—look almost new. The body of Devine has not been found."

"Rugs almost new, eh?" Strang's head worked up and down. "Perhaps they are new. As for Devine, the Senator and Quinn are quite able to take care of their own dead. When my story—my evidence—is no longer a danger to Quinn Devine's body will show up."

"And when will that be?"

"When I am dead."

"Nice talk." Barton pounded the floor again. "But that evidence. Why in hell, if you have it, don't you give it to me? We could pick up Quinn—chance a squeal just as you suggested. If you have it, why don't you give it to me?"

Mr. Strang looked at the Inspector for a full minute. Then he spoke.

"For the first time in my life I am unable to make a decision. I don't know why I don't give it to you. I don't know why." And suddenly staring at the clock, "It's after one and she hasn't called—something may have happened to her."

"Nonsense!" Barton stopped for a moment, then, seeing the real anxiety in Strang's face, said, "As a matter of fact she'll be a little late tonight."

"Why?" Strang snapped.

"Because," Barton said easily, "she is robbing a house."

And before Strang could break into a tirade, "She told me. She said the house she is robbing is pretty well watched. There is an envelope of great importance that Quinn wants. She thinks, from what he said, it concerns Senator Stone— maybe even divulged his whereabouts." He moved broad shoulders. "I trust the girl, sent down word to a couple of plainclothesmen in the neighborhood, and tipped off the harness bull on the corner not to even see her if she jumped out of a window and landed on their shoulders."

"She seems to trust you a good deal, Inspector," Strang said.

"Sure, and you don't like it? You've treated her like a stepchild—and she's in love with you."

"She told you that?"

"She didn't need to," said Barton. "I'm not that dumb. She's in a hurry to finish up things—in a hurry to get that bullet out of your head."

"I haven't seen her in days." Strang breathed more easily.

"Well," said Barton, "what about that evidence? Don't you see the danger? Any day Quinn will suspect—and just like that—" He ran a hand across his throat suggestively. "Hell, man, even if the Senator is guilty, which he isn't, Quinn will squawk all over his face like any other rat. So, why not give me the papers?"

"Because," said Strang slowly, "I'm not quite sure Quinn can squeal."

Barton said:

"And the girl. She's in danger of a sudden death every minute of the day and night—a horrible death."

"I have told her to drop out of things."

"But she's in it for you, to save you, to clean up things before you get knocked off or go nuts."

"I told her," said Strang again, and his face was very grim, "to stay out of things."

"By God!" said Barton, who wanted that evidence and didn't altogether believe there was any. "That won't bring her back to life."

STRANG CAME SLOWLY to his feet, walked across to the desk in the corner of his library, pulled out a drawer and laid it on the floor. Then, stretching his hand in full length, he opened a small safe. Inside this safe, in an even deeper compartment which looked like the safe itself, he produced the tightly folded papers. He was stretching up with them when Barton spoke.

"Funny about Resa Kent's job tonight—and lucky she stood in with me. A stoolie rang up and gave me the dope that Resa Kent would rob that house at about twelve. Don't look so surprised. He said he was a friend of yours."

Strang said sharply:

"What do you mean by that? I have no stoolies—no friends. No one in the underworld serves me now that Simon Becker is dead."

"Maybe a lad of Becker's. He said he knew Becker and thought Becker would like you to know. Hell, he wanted me to promise not to tell you he called." Barton rubbed his chin. "And that was funny, because he said he called you at your home here and couldn't reach you."

Strang ran a hand through his hair. He had never mentioned Resa Kent to Simon Becker. But it was true that Becker had mentioned her to him, more than once in his information about Quinn. Yes, he remembered now, once in particular Simon Becker had said that there was going to be an awful bust-up when Quinn tossed over Gertie Bender for the "Kent dame."

"Don't get it at all, eh?" Barton looked at him. "What difference does it make? Probably a lad working for Simon saw a chance to pick up with you and tossed me the bone. Stoolies are funny. I promised him a century for the squeal, told him to say nothing, and that I'd pick up the girl okay."

"But Simon Becker had my orders to mention my name to no one."

"Ain't that too cute," Barton kidded. "I'd like to have a buck for every lad I know who disobeyed my orders."

"I paid him well," Strang said, "and promised him everything. I even promised him death."

"Why worry over that." Barton walked toward Strang. "Let me have a slant at those papers, and I'll believe the pipe dream of yours about the unconscious Senator and the dead Charlie Devine."

"Here—" He held out the folded sheets. "It's yours. If Martin Quinn can talk and does my mission is complete. If he does not—then I have failed."

Barton took the papers. Strang sat, his head buried in his hands. He liked to think it was the bullet in his brain that made him the beaten man he now felt he was. He liked to tell himself that it was the physical not the mental or the spiritual that had beaten him. But he knew the truth— knew it even as he denied it.

Resa Kent had rushed to him just as he was about to murder a man. Not kill him—but murder him—shoot him to death as he lay upon the floor. He had killed men— quite a few men. He had sent many more to prison, and perhaps a dozen to their death in the chair. But he had never murdered a man. The phone rang in the little room adjoining the library.

Strang came wearily to his feet and looked at Inspector Barton. But Barton's attention was fastened upon those papers. His eyes were wide. His mouth hung open. Martin Quinn, the great Quinn, was in the bag.

Mr. Strang, the man who had, for a while, struck terror into the members of the underworld, seemed a bent old man as he moved across to the little room. The phone rang again. He straightened slightly, his step was just a bit quicker. This would be Resa Kent and meant she was safe. Just one thing now. He would ask her to come to him—tell her he needed her. Would she believe it just a ruse to get her there—get her out of danger? It was the truth, he did need her. He was a broken man—a useless man—and he needed her.

8

A KILLER IN THE NIGHT

STRANG LIFTED THE phone. An eagerness crept into his usual hard voice.

He said: "Strang Cummings speaking."

"Strang Cummings, eh?" said a loud, rather cheerful voice. "Why I'm looking for the bad boy of the night. The bad boy who was going to clear up the troubles of the laws. Martin Quinn talking."

"Quinn—Martin Quinn!" Strang stammered.

"Don't seem your old self tonight." The voice of Quinn that he recognized quite easily now went on: "I'll cheer you up. That little girl friend—that little girl who loves you—you know, Resa Kent—" The cheerful, good humor went out of Quinn's voice and a hardness crept in. "Well, I just busted her right in the teeth—right smack in the teeth."

"Yes," said Strang. He seemed dazed.

"And at a bad time, too. I just gave another girl the air. Funny the things you learn, Strang, when you tell a woman to walk out. Hell, she had thought up so many things about my past life. Yep, that dumb cluck had a memory I never imagined she had. She forgot about furs, jewelry, that sort of stuff—and raked up my past. Of course, not a past that would equal that fine bunch of papers you have, but a past—well, you're a man of the world. Women talk as long as they can. But she'll never talk again after tonight."

And Strang didn't know how those words, after the more terrifying ones that followed, would burn themselves into his mind later. *She'll never talk again after tonight.*

"Well," Quinn went on, "the Senator and I have Resa Kent. She looks strong. She looks healthy. She looks as if she might live a bit. Of course I'm not as young as I used to be, and I might get tired. Get the point? She's to be tortured to death, unless—"

"Unless—" Strang said. No thoughts seemed to be in his head—just a pounding there.

"Boy," said Quinn, misunderstanding the evident indifference, "I'll say this for her—though we haven't really started to work on her yet. She won't trap you—at least our way. When I smacked her around a bit she flashed a damned ugly temper. Said she loved you and chucked it in our faces. I was wondering how you felt about her."

"Just what do you mean?"

"Oh, I was thinking you might bring those papers to me for the girl's life. I know you haven't turned them over to Barton yet, or he'd have acted. He's built that way. There's no hurry, boy, if you want to think it over—that is, if she's as strong as she looks and her heart holds out. Of course, the more I look at her the more steamed up I get. Been making a monkey out of me. I could shove the tongs smack in both her rotten, brown eyes."

"Rotten, brown eyes—" Strang started in a daze. Then he suddenly seemed to snap out of it. He said quickly:

"Barton hasn't got that evidence about you. I have. I'll turn it in for the girl. What do you want me to do?"

"Do? Right away, you mean? Want to keep her face pretty, eh?"

"Right away," said Strang. "Right now."

"Good!" Quinn's voice was surprised, though he tried to hide that. "The fact is I didn't think you'd come around so quick. But I'll have a car, a black sedan, laying up at Sunnyside and Eighth, uptown side, east. It'll be there in an hour."

"And the assurance of her safety?"

"My word," said Quinn. "The word of Martin Quinn that has never been broken." And if he thought of the same words he had spoken to Simon Becker just the minute before he shot him to death it did not show in his voice.

"Just that, eh?" Strang said. "But how do I know she's there—you really have her?"

MARTIN QUINN CHUCKLED pleasantly.

"You can thank your dear friend, Inspector Barton, for that. I was told the girl was a two-timing little tart. I didn't believe it, but I put her to a test. I gave her a job to do—a bit of house-breaking—then had Barton tipped she was going to do it. And did Barton arrest her and take the letter she obtained for me? He did not. He even cleared the block to make it easier for her. Try to picture the greeting I gave her when she walked in with that envelope in her hand."

"I see," Strang said. "I'm to come with the evidence you wish and she leaves?"

"You'll come unarmed, of course. If you monkey with the police you'll be shot to death and the police will get no information. The men in the first car that picks you up won't know where she is, so they won't know where the boys in the second car will take you."

"Just your word that she goes free." Strang hardly more than whispered the words.

A sudden scream—a scream that seemed forced through tightly held lips—a cry of sudden agony came to Strang's ear over the phone. Then Quinn's gruff order as he evidently turned his head from the phone. "Lay off that dame, Walt, I'm making a deal and putting it through right." And his voice back over the wire to Strang again: "Sorry about the interruption, Mr. Strang. Well, what do you say?"

Mr. Strang said simply:

"I'll be there with the evidence."

He waited a moment, heard the click over the wire. It was with an effort he came to his feet. There was little evidence without those papers. They were, to a great extent, in the form of affidavits, signed statements—even finger prints.

Strang walked slowly from the room. His foot hadn't passed over the door jamb before Inspector Barton spoke; spoke without looking up.

"You've done the trick, Strang. I never hoped for anything like this. I thought it would take weeks, maybe months going back over this information to build up a case. But it's—" He looked up as Strang walked toward him. "Good God, man, what's the matter with you? Seen a ghost?"

Strang took the papers from Barton's hand and folded them before placing them in his jacket pocket. He just looked at Barton with dull, listless eyes.

Barton came slowly to his feet.

"What's happened?" he demanded.

Strang stretched out his right hand and flattened it on

the table for support. "I am taking that evidence—to give to Quinn. I'm not blaming you, Barton. You couldn't have known. Quinn fooled the girl. Pretended he wanted her to pull a job—had someone phone you she was doing it. When she wasn't arrested he knew the truth. Now he's going to kill her, kill her slowly, torture her to death if I don't—"

"So you're taking that evidence to Quinn. Is that it?" Barton moved slightly forward, then stepped back before the open door. "Don't be a fool, Strang! He'll just kill the girl and you and come back to hunt again in the city. You know he wouldn't keep his word and let you both go free!"

"No, I know that." Strang nodded. "But there would be no need to torture her then; to keep her there in a living hell. God! Don't you see? Don't you understand, I've got to go!"

"For the girl, eh?" Barton edged to the door, blocking his way. "Why a few minutes ago the girl was forgotten. You've never had anything but a mission. Don't tell me you've gone soft—gone yellow."

"Is it yellow to die like that?" Strang asked suddenly.

"I don't mean that, Strang. I don't mean that. Something's come over you. Hundreds of lives are at stake— thousands of them over the years. Your connection with the underworld has gone. I won't let you go." And as Strang walked slowly toward him, bent, tired, his feet shuffling: "Where's the years of vengeance now? Where's the mission? Where's the Mr. Strang who was a machine? Where's the little boy who saw his father killed and—"

"Stop! Stop!" Strang cried. "Can't you see? Can't you understand! I'm not the same man. The man who was a machine. The man who was walking death in the night. The man who hardly believed himself to be human is in love with a woman." Strang stopped close to the door. A sudden change came over him.

STRANG SUDDENLY STRAIGHTENED his shoulders. He was suddenly many inches taller. And the thing was in his eyes again. It was blazing there.

"No—no—" Barton grabbed for his gun, had it half out when Strang struck with the back of his hand. It did not seem a hard blow. Did not seem to come from a great distance, but the strength was there. Barton was a strong man, yet he was thrown back—smashed against the wall. He slid downward and sat upon the floor. Barton may have told himself that he was too dazed to shoot; too dazed to pull that gun the rest of the way from its holster. But he wasn't. He just didn't, that was all. He listened and heard Strang say:

"Gertie Bender, Martin Quinn's woman. Where does she live?"

And Barton answered:

"The Raven Gardens Apartments; has the penthouse upstairs." Barton stared at Strang. His mouth hung open. His eyes popped slightly. A minute ago he had thought Strang a broken man. What he saw now made him shudder slightly—not in fear—but in horror.

"All right," Mr. Strang was saying. "You want a man of vengeance, a man of hate, a man with the lust to maim and kill and torture. You want just what you're getting—a mad man. I know many of Quinn's people. I know where they sleep, where they eat, where they drink."

"What do you mean?" Barton just gasped the words. His gun was clutched in his hand now.

"I mean that a mad killer stalks the underworld tonight." Strang laughed and it was loud and shrill. "You'll have to hold me for murder, Barton, after tonight. I thought I feared madness. Well, I'll glory in it tonight. By breakfast time Quinn will wish he'd never laid a hand on that girl." He tapped his pocket. "You may find this evidence on my dead body possibly, but I'll need a lot of killing tonight." Then, before Barton could speak he was gone. Feet beat across the hall. Somewhere far distant in the darkness of that house a door closed.

In that room, gun in hand, stood Barton. He reeled toward the table. Then he spilled the first glass of whisky he had ever spilled either drunk or sober, downed the second without its customary water and shook his head. He picked up the telephone and called Sergeant Grant—his friend of twenty years.

He was wondering very seriously if he did right in not shooting Strang when he had had the opportunity.

9

MR. STRANG TAKES A RIDE

IF IT WAS a mad man who had left that house, it was not apparent to the casual strangers who still walked the streets of the city. They saw only a tall, lean figure whose face was hardly visible.

Strang walked with his usual steady step. His face was set as tightly as it often had been on so many of these early morning journeys. He thumbed a passing taxi, gave a downtown address and sat easily back in the cab. So it had come at last, had it? He laughed slightly. So this was madness; the madness that he had feared? And now that it had come, there was nothing alarming about it. Nothing different. He was simply going out into the night to kill men. Kill men who worked for Martin Quinn.

He leaned forward suddenly and spoke to the driver. He spoke simply, sharply. The cab turned around and drove uptown.

The penthouse that Gertie Bender occupied was on the roof of the smart Raven Gardens Apartments. It contained nine rooms, a little terrace along the front facing on the river, and a sunken garden that ran from the entrance of the bungalow itself to the main door which led to stairs and so to the elevators below. It had comfort and privacy. Gertie was enjoying neither of these at the moment.

She sat stiff and straight and wide-eyed in her modern living room. She had been sitting that way for sometime. One man had taken up his position outside the door, while the other searched diligently about the room, a heavy forty-five hanging in his right hand. Finally he opened a tiny, half-hidden drawer in the desk, fumbled steadily about, drew out a twenty-five automatic, and turned back to the girl.

Gertie knew the man all right. She knew the stories about him along the Avenue. Harry Davidson never charged one penny more for knocking over a woman than he did a man. She said to Davidson—though her lips curved into a defiance, there was both a trembling to her lips and to her words:

"What's the reason, Harry? Why my gun? If you've got to do it, why not the big cannon?" She nodded at the gun he had just slipped beneath his arm. "It'll take a couple or three of them little pellets to do it. You haven't anything against me, Harry."

Harry Davidson shrugged his shoulders.

"It's Quinn's way, kid," he said. "You double-crossed him."

The girl's eyes widened as the man walked about the room, his eyes never off her. He slipped on a pair of gloves before he filled the glass with whisky and tossed it into the fireplace. Then he hurled a few pillows about, sprinkled whisky generously around, laid the bottle on its side on the table so that the liquor leaked out, ran along the table and splashed upon a thousand dollar rug.

"The dirty rat!" Gertie didn't exactly blast out the words. It wasn't left in her to do that. "I played straight with him. I could have had him fried to a crisp if I'd ever opened my yap. I should have guessed it. He didn't want me to have visitors until lately—when he let me go back in the show business. Then he told me it was good for business to have the right people come here; money in his pocket and mine. Said maybe I'd wake up some morning a star. Yeah, Quinn was playing the new dame then. Building up my out. Fixing soft guys and big names in town so the cops would soft-pedal a scandal. He—" She stopped, lit a cigarette with trembling fingers, held it to her lips. Her fingers shook and her face was white—a yellowish white. Finally she said:

"You're not a louse, Harry. Give me a break—I could lay my hands on a few grand when the banks open."

Harry Davidson half raised his gun.

"It's your life or mine. Tough, but you dames never see ahead!" There was no rancor in Harry's voice.

"Okay." She stiffened, gripped the arms of the chair. "I know Quinn. I know that it would be your life if you don't take mine. Fire away."

Harry Davidson raised his gun, started to close his finger on the trigger and the girl screamed. She couldn't control that. Sheer terror was in her voice, in her eyes. And that scream hid the single cry outside the room. But it didn't hide the fall of the body—the crash of a heavy man upon the floor.

The girl's scream stopped as if an unseen hand pressed against her mouth. Harry Davidson swung, raised his gun. There was a single shot but it did not come from Davidson's gun. Davidson simply gave at the knees and sank slowly to the floor.

Davidson had not stretched himself full length upon that floor before a figure was stepping over his body. A man whose eyes were twin lights. And the man spoke; spoke as he held the gun almost against her chest. A gun that still smelt of burnt powder. The man said:

"Quinn put up your number. I took it down. I want to kill him tonight. Can you tell me where to find him?"

The woman tried to speak—had to close her eyes to block out the burning eyes that seemed to hypnotize her. She finally said:

"You bet I can. And I know his racket too, and—"

"I simply want to know where Quinn and the girl are."

It was less than five minutes later that Mr. Strang led the trembling girl through the servants' entrance. He said:

"Go straight to my place." And he gave her the number. "A Chinese will let you in. Say Mr. Strang sent you. In the morning, if I do not return, tell your story to Inspector Barton. Here." He slipped a Chinese coin into her hand. "Give the Chinese that. He will understand and let you in."

Then Strang was gone. For some time Gertie Bender stood on the pavement, then she turned and ran in swift panic down a dark side street. Gertie Bender was hard; everyone knew that. Yet she had to hold her hand across her mouth to keep from shrieking. She had looked, down into a man's eyes, and she had seen something horrible there.

10

DEATH FOR TWO

MARTIN QUINN STOOD in the pleasant, second-floor living room and looked at the light curtains before the wide, French windows that gave off the tiny balcony. Then he looked over at Resa Kent who sat on the couch and faced him. They were the only two in that room. Martin Quinn said:

"A guy hates to be wrong about a woman, though he nearly always is. But I had an idea you were class and would be straight."

The girl said:

"That's why you were so easily fooled. You wouldn't recognize 'class' and you wouldn't understand what a word like 'straight' meant. You couldn't see that a girl like me would feel it way down in the pit of her stomach when you even put a hand on her shoulder. It's not pleasant to play in the dirt."

Quinn jerked up his head, then grinned. He had heard that stuff before, but not exactly in the same way. Men and women both. But when he put the screws on them, they played a different tune. What he hated most, and what seemed to pierce his thick hide was the contempt in her face, the difference in her voice.

"Do you know," Quinn said, "I've got some of the boys downstairs? I have a good mind to kid our famous Mr. Strang along. Let him think I'm really going to let you go. Then I'll let him watch you die. He'll sit right in that chair there and watch you die."

"You said that before," the girl told him.

"Did I?" Beady eyes tightened to such tiny points of blackness as to make them just visible in the yellow whiteness. "But I didn't say how you'll die. You double-crossed me. Strang killed my men. There were Johnny Lester, Steve Blake, and damn' near a half dozen others. And you trapped them to their deaths. Death can sometimes be pretty horrible, Miss Resa Kent."

"There could be things more horrible, I guess."

"For instance?" His lips curled.

"The penthouse, the furs and the Rolls." The girl laughed and succeeded fairly well in keeping the hysteria out of it.

Quinn lifted a great hand; took a step forward; stopped.

"Get up," he ordered, and when she did not move: "Get up if you've got the stomach to stand and face me."

Resa Kent came slowly to her feet, took two steps forward and looked him straight in the eyes. She never raised a hand when he struck her; crashed his open, right hand to her cheek, knocking her across the room, onto the floor against the couch. She struggled to her knees. Her head swam. But she didn't cry out, and she didn't put her hand to her aching cheek. She staggered to the couch and sat down.

Martin Quinn's lips quivered in anger. It was just the same when he had so brutally beaten her before he carried her to the car. She had not even cried out.

"We'll see," he said, "how you like it when your lover comes."

THE GIRL TRIED to smile. It hurt, but she got the words out.

"That's one thing I don't have to worry about. I love Strang. I love him enough to die for him. Love him enough to never make a plea across a telephone wire that might bring him here. He won't come. He can't come. He's a man with a mission." Her voice raised louder. "He's a man with a madness and that madness is to get you. He's got evidence that will burn you and he'll hunt you as he would a mad dog. He can't come to save me. His work is to save thousands of others. Do you hear me, Martin Quinn? It's you he wants. It's you he's hunted for years. He's Robert Kenyon, the boy with the bullet in his head. The little boy who would have put the finger on you long ago."

Quinn's face blanched.

"I know it. I know it now," he said. "And you knew that all along?"

"All along," said the girl. "I'm Resa Hastings. I'm the daughter of the District Attorney you had murdered."

"Like that, eh?" Quinn's face was still white. "So you worked together. I knew about the boy—knew it then. I didn't know about you."

"Nor did Mr. Strang," the girl said. "Nor does he know now. I wasn't born then—not until some months after my father's death. When that boy grew up, he wrote letters to my mother. There was never any address; just words of hate, of vengeance. She could not answer them, and they continued to come after she died. Each one a mounting hate—each one the promise of vengeance. A vengeance that finally turned into a justice. An obsession to free the entire state from a great wrong—Parole. And that final letter, when he was ready to strike. The letter he said would be his last. He said the papers would soon carry the name of Mr. Strang and that you would hear the name of Mr. Strang and fear it."

The girl stopped for breath, then continued:

"And you hear it and fear it. Not only fear Mr. Strang, but you now fear the entire city police—the state police. The entire forces of the nation will hunt you down." And in a quieter voice, "The evil of Parole will be corrected. Therefore, what can my life matter?"

Martin Quinn walked toward her; this time his huge hand closed into a fist.

"He'll come. He said he'd come." And yet, as Quinn raised his fist strike the girl, he was afraid. The Mr. Strang he had known, tried to eliminate—had learned to fear—was not the man to give his life for a woman.

Footsteps on the stairs! Quinn dropped his fist, turned to the door as it burst open. Two men were there. One carried a machine gun beneath his arm. They spoke together—quick, hurried voices.

Quinn cursed.

"You, Walt," he said to the biggest of the two men. "What is it? What is it?"

"Mr. Strang!" The man called Walt tightened his hold on the Tommy gun. "He's on his way here. Pete and Macy showed up in the car. Strang didn't meet them. And Gertie isn't dead. She has disappeared. But Harry Davidson is dead—and Joe. God! He crushed his skull with the butt of a gun as if it was an eggshell."

"Joe dead?"

"Deader than hell. The elevator man brought Strang up. Frank Hogan brought the word to us uptown. We came straight here."

"Where's Hogan now?" Quinn demanded, Hogan was Walt's friend.

"He took a run-out powder, Boss. He must have walked into that penthouse right after the killing. I was waiting at the drugstore like you said and got Hogan's call. You can't blame him, Boss. He said Davidson was—well, just dead, but that Joe was a mess."

QUINN JERKED A gun into his hand—looked frantically around the room. It was getting him too. Panic was in the air. Walt was urging him to beat it. The car was outside. Quinn gripped himself, said:

"If Gertie told him the place, he'd be here by this time."

"Hardly," Walt argued. "He'd come the long way, of course. If he went for the cops he'll be some time yet."

Quinn said:

"He won't go for the cops. He'll come alone. Quick! How many are here?"

"I've got the typewriter." He patted the machine gun. "Pete is here with me. Tony and Abrams are down by the car. Then there's Fergy with the Senator."

"All right," said Quinn. "Strang will come alone. I'm sure of that. You go downstairs, Walt, and tell Tony to wait just down the lane with the car. Abrams can take the front of the house and you the back." He hesitated, looked at the machine gun. "No, let Pete tell the boys, and take the back himself. You stay here, Walt."

Six armed men and the Senator made seven. At least
one of those men had a machine gun. And they knew fear.

Resa Kent watched the two men quietly. The color came
back to her cheeks. Her brown eyes sparkled. She didn't
think of Quinn—of the evidence—of the Parole Evil now.
She thought only of Strang. Strang was coming to fight
for her!

Quinn was still giving orders, calling down the stairs.
Then he closed the door after Pete, looked over at Walt,
nodded at the sub-machine gun and laughed—a rather
false laugh.

"Now, we're ready for Mr. Strang. I'm only sorry I can't
meet him here in this room alone."

There was just the slightest tremor in his voice, but the
sensitive ears of the girl heard it. She said:

"You wouldn't meet him alone tonight for all the money
in the world."

This time it was Quinn's fist that caught her and knocked
her into the corner. But the blow had come a long way
before it hit her. She sat there; still conscious but not quite
able to rise. And there was a smile on her bleeding lips.

Then things happened so suddenly that the girl who was
staring directly at that window did not see the slightest
movement of curtains or hear the slightest sound before
it happened.

It was just one single, great crash. The French doors with
their little square windows burst into the room tearing the
curtains before them, scattering glass all about. There was
a cry from Quinn as his gun shot into his hand. And Resa
saw Strang. Hate—vengeance—hardness—cruelty—all
that was terrible in man she saw there on the face of the

man she loved. And too, more back in his eyes, a vicious lust to kill.

Just for a second he bent double as he stumbled into the room and she saw the two guns in his hands as he straightened. Then it came. Came from over close to the door. The sudden horrifying and deadly, staccato notes of the machine gun.

She saw Strang's body tremble and closed her eyes. She knew that was the end. Even with her eyes closed she could feel each thud of the bullet as it entered his body.

11

MR. STRANG IN PERSON

THEN A SINGLE roar that seemed louder than the others, and the sudden silence of the machine gun. She knew that Strang must be dead. After that, a split-second of silence and then a laugh. A horrible, eerie laugh. She opened her eyes. Mr. Strang stood there swaying on his feet. Stood there, his burning eyes upon the popping ones of Martin Quinn. In the corner by the door Walt, the gunner, lay. He didn't move.

She saw Quinn's hand shake and saw the yellow-blue flame dart from the end of his gun. She heard, too, a picture a good five feet to the right of Strang, crash to the floor.

Both his guns raised and covered Martin Quinn. Mr. Strang spoke.

"Ten feet—not over ten feet." Strang nodded his head up and down as he swayed there before Quinn. "And you couldn't make it. I knew you couldn't make it. Well, Martin Quinn, I've come for the girl, and I've come for you."

A trembling finger of Martin Quinn tightened and Strang shot. Martin Quinn's right hand fell to his side. He leaned over and tried to grip the gun with his left. There was another single roar. Martin Quinn raised his left hand and tore at the hole in his chest.

Resa Kent ran across to the door, locked it. She cried out: "Don't, Strang! Not like that. There are others below."

She turned just as Quinn jerked up that left hand and fired. She didn't know whether he hit Strang or not. She couldn't tell. Strang's face and chest were covered with blood. But she saw Strang fire just once, and saw Martin Quinn's head drop on his chest. It was rather terrible watching death in Quinn's eyes.

She realized when she grabbed Strang how many times he must have been hit by the machine gun. She realized, too, just how near death he must be. And she heard the pounding of feet below, the calling of men. Then she heard Strang speak. Somehow it was as if he spoke to her through the large end of a megaphone. The words didn't seem to come from his lips at all.

"The big chair there—by the bookcase," Strang said as he staggered forward, and she kept him from falling. "My back so—" He leaned against the bookcase. His knees gave, and she had to steady him, had to put her hands upon his body. She could feel it twitch with pain.

"The chair—the chair." He just panted the words. Heavy feet beat across the hall without. A gun roared. Wood split in the door. For the first time the girl realized what Strang wanted. Despite his wounds, despite his madness he had taken up a position in the room where no bullet fired blindly through the door could hit him, nor could a shot come directly at him through the broken windows.

She never knew how she did it. And she was not thinking of herself as great tears rolled down her cheeks. For the first and almost certainly the last time, she was obeying his orders to the letter.

He wanted the chair to lean upon to keep him from falling. She had to lift his arms one at a time upon the back
of that huge chair. Arms that he was unable to lift, yet his
fingers still clutched the guns.

BOTH HIS ARMS upon that chair and guns clutched tightly
in his hands—his body forward, his feet braced against the
bookcase—he turned his head and said to the girl:

"I came for you, Resa—not for my mission. I want you to
know it was for you." And after a moment when she didn't
answer, "You're crying. Your lips are moving but I can't hear
what you're saying."

"I'm—I'm praying, Strang," she said. "I'm praying—"

Strang interrupted. His voice was weak. A great body
had hurled itself against the door. The wood was cracking.

"Pray," Strang said, "that Senator Stone will be the first
to enter that door."

Another smash against the door and Strang sagged.
Frantically his brain tried to send messages to his hands.
But that brain failed the left hand. Plainly he saw his
fingers open—plainly he saw the gun topple from his hand
land upon the chair. The right hand. The right gun—

And the door burst open.

"Stone—Senator Stone!" Strang's rang with triumph.
His right shot up and the gun fell from limp fingers, fell as
he looked straight into the eyes of the man he had hoped
to kill.

Something else after that. Inspector Barton was there.
Uniformed men. Barton explaining that Gertie Bender
had telephoned him. And Senator Stone holding Strang
and talking—strange, queer words but Strang had enough
of them.

"I've been a fool—a real fool," the Senator was saying. "Why, Quinn donated close to a hundred thousand dollars toward the secret investigation of the Parole System. I'm to blame for all this. Quinn told me—he blamed everything on you. He was helping me to investigate you. I did speak to Barton about you, but he laughed at me. It was then that I sent for you to warn you from the city. I didn't wish to make my investigation public and I wanted to study you myself. God in Heaven! I brought all this suffering on the young lady and—"

Barton was lifting Strang to the couch. He said:

"The Senator was a fool with a laudable purpose. He knew the truth after he found your note when he came to, that night you killed Charlie Devine. Martin Quinn walked in while he was reading it. That's how the Senator happened to be a prisoner here. You see, Quinn built up a feeling that a big influence was behind him. He never actually admitted it—in fact, denied it. But that made it all the stronger—put him in stronger with the right people too."

Barton was talking when Strang lost consciousness. And it was days later when he heard Barton talking again.

Barton was saying to the surgeon: "And the bullet was in his brain. My God! You removed nearly half the brain and he'll live?"

The doctor answered:

"He'll live and be sane. Such an operation was always possible. It's just that it took time to get around to it. What we scoffed at yesterday is scientific fact today. He'll live and be normal. It was really his condition that made the operation so nearly fatal. Those machine gun slugs. We can't expect miracles. It'll take weeks—there were seventeen blood transfusions, you know, Commissioner."

AND ALL STRANG got from that conversation was that Barton was now Commissioner of Police, that he had lost half his brain, and that he was using the other half to think of Resa Kent.

The next time he opened his eyes he saw Resa. Her head was very close, her hair touched his cheek, and someone in white whom he wasn't able to curse at led her away.

It was long after that, and Strang was able to use both his arms when Resa sat on the bed and told him about herself. Barton came in while she was there.

"I've got great news for you, Strang." Barton stuck to the name. "Senator Stone is burnt up at himself and with the Governor's backing is presenting a bill to the Legislature. There, there, I know he's an old fool, but he's a sincere one."

"If Quinn was able to make a fool out of him *what* a Parole Bill his will be!"

"Oh, I don't know." Barton stroked his chin. "If the right sort of lad wrote it up for him. You see, the Senator is well thought of. I've sort of encouraged the talk around that you were really working for him in the investigation. It's made Senator Stone quite a man."

"Yes?" Strang said. "And what did it make me?"

"You—well, the Senator would very much like to have you write up the bill." And gripping Strang's hand as Resa came back to the side of the bed. "No need to ask if you're mad now." Barton walked toward the door, turned back and jerked a thumb at the girl. "I was just as mad myself twenty-two years ago come next Tuesday."